How to plant a tree:

① Decide what kind of tree to plant.

② Contact your state conservation department or a local nursery for ideas.

③ Dig a hole as big as the tree's root ball.

④ Plant, cover, and then water deeply.

Plant a tree. Leave a legacy! Nature _and_ nurture!

P9-CFF-256

OAK LAWN PUBLIC LIBRARY

3 1186 00876 7352

960L

REGARDING THE TREES

Other books in this series by
Kate Klise and M. Sarah Klise:

Regarding the Fountain:
A Tale, in Letters, of Liars and Leaks

Regarding the Sink:
Where, Oh Where, Did Waters Go?

Regarding the Bathrooms:
A Privy to the Past

Regarding the Bees:
A Lesson, in Letters, on Honey,
Dating, and Other Sticky Subjects

REGARDING THE TREES

A Splintered Saga Rooted in Secrets

KATE KLISE

Illustrated by M. SARAH KLISE

FEB 2 3 2015
OAK LAWN LIBRARY

sandpiper

HOUGHTON MIFFLIN HARCOURT

Boston New York

Text copyright © 2005 by Kate Klise
Illustrations copyright © 2005 by M. Sarah Klise

All rights reserved. Published in the United States by Sandpiper, an imprint
of Houghton Mifflin Harcourt Publishing Company. Originally published in
hardcover in the United States by Harcourt Children's Books, an imprint
of Houghton Mifflin Harcourt Publishing Company, 2005.

SANDPIPER and the SANDPIPER logo are trademarks
of Houghton Mifflin Harcourt Publishing Company.

For information about permission to reproduce selections from this book,
write to Permissions, Houghton Mifflin Harcourt Publishing Company,
215 Park Avenue South, New York, New York 10003.

Classroom activities first appeared online in the Regarding the . . . series
Teacher's Guide at www.HarcourtBooks.com, 2007.

www.sandpiperbooks.com

The Library of Congress has cataloged the hardcover edition as follows:
Klise, Kate.
Regarding the trees: a splintered saga rooted in secrets/by Kate Klise;
illustrated by M. Sarah Klise.
p.   cm. — (Regarding the— ; 3)
Summary: In this story told primarily through letters, Principal Russ wants the middle school
trees to be trimmed before his administrative evaluation, but the project is interrupted by a
town gender war, dueling chefs, student tree protests, and a surprise wedding.
[1. Trees—Fiction.   2. Schools—Fiction.   3. School principals—Fiction.
4. Letters—Fiction.   5. Humorous stories.]   I. Klise, M. Sarah, ill.   II. Title.   III. Series.
PZ7.K684Rega   2005
[Fic]—dc22   2004027211
ISBN 978-0-15-205163-1
ISBN 978-0-15-206090-9 pb

Designed by M. Sarah Klise with assistance from
Barry Age and Matthew Willis

DOC 15 14 13 12 11
4500430268
Printed in the United States of America

*This is a work of fiction. All the characters in this book are the product of the
author's and the illustrator's imaginations. Although no sixth-grade students
were harmed, and no principals got the ax in the creation of this story, a few trees
did make a noble sacrifice. And so we salute the very nonfictional trees that
inspire us to grow while staying grounded—and that have become the pages you
hold in your hands in the form of a book.*

This book is dedicated to our
*tree*mendous nephew
Lorenzo von Zerneck.

If you want to be happy for a year, plant a garden;
if you want to be happy for life, plant a tree.

—English proverb

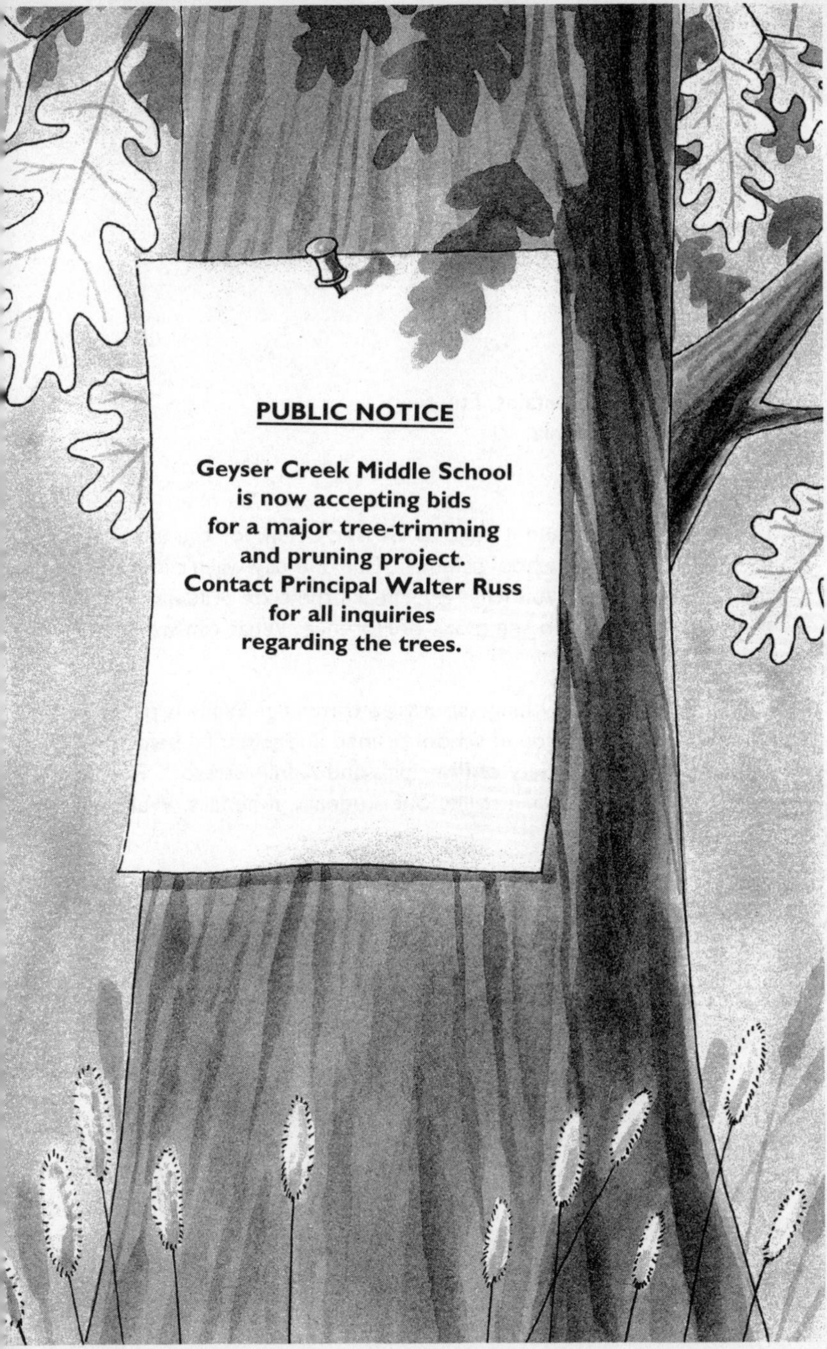
PUBLIC NOTICE
Geyser Creek Middle School is now accepting bids for a major tree-trimming and pruning project. Contact Principal Walter Russ for all inquiries regarding the trees.

From the Desk of Goldie Fisch

March 28

Florence Waters
President
Flowing Waters Fountains, Etc.
Watertown, California

Dear Florence,

I was so glad you made it back to Geyser Creek for the unveiling of the new sink in the school cafeteria. But one day wasn't long enough for your visit! After you left, I overheard the sixth graders saying they'd give *anything* to see more of Florence. What can we do to get you back here?

Say, do you know anything about tree trimming? Wally is pining to get all the trees around school pruned and trimmed before his evaluation by the Society of Principals and Administrators. Principals have to pass tests, too, just like our students. If he fails, Wally will get fired.

I'm not exactly sure what Wally has in mind regarding the trees. I'll find out.

Sincerely,

Goldie

Goldie Fisch

P.S. I can't wait to taste Chef Angelo's cooking! A real Italian chef, right here at Geyser Creek Middle School. What a wonderful gift!

P.P.S. And because I know you'll ask: Sam N. and I have another date this week. I need some advice, please!

Watertown, California

March 31

Goldie Fisch
The Woman Who Knows (and Does!) Everything at...
Geyser Creek Middle School
Geyser Creek, Missouri

Pure Goldie,

Of course the students—and you!—should see Florence.
Of all the cities in Italy, it's my favorite.

I'll make sure the children see Florence in person.
That's a promise—and a secret. Don't tell anyone, okay?

Here's another promise: You will *love* Angelo's cooking.
He's one of the best chefs I've ever met. Of course, your
sister Angel's food at Geyser Creek Cafe is heavenly, too!

Now, regarding the trees: I've never pruned a tree before.
(Golly, it sounds like fun!) But I've planted and trimmed
thousands of trees in my life. I'm rather good at it, if I
do say so myself.

I'll wait to hear from Wally. Remember not to write his
letters for him. We wouldn't want him to fail his evaluation, would we? If Wally was ever fired, who would we
tease?

Your friend,

Florence

P.S. Oh! About your date with Sam N.: Be yourself. And
dine at the most romantic spot you can find.

Goldie, you know I'm rooting
for you and Sam!

GEYSER CREEK MIDDLE SCHOOL
Geyser Creek, Missouri
Our NEW school motto: *Go with the Flo!*

Mr. Walter Russ
Principal

OVERNIGHT MAIL

April 1

Ms. Florence Waters
President
Flowing Waters Fountains, Etc.
Watertown, California

Dear Ms. Waters,

As you might have noticed on your recent visit to Geyser Creek, the trees on our school campus have become quite overgrown. One tree in particular, a giant weeping willow behind the school, is in need of serious pruning, if not total elimination. The remaining hundred or so trees require trimming.

I can't imagine you have the experience, expertise, or necessary equipment for a tree-trimming project of this magnitude. Then again, I've learned better than to assume anything when it comes to you, Ms. Waters. If you would like to bid on this tree-trimming and pruning job, please advise soonest.

As part of my yearly evaluation by the Society of Principals and Administrators, I will be graded on the appearance of our school campus, as well as on how I award and administer contracts for projects such as this.

In the past, evaluators have reviewed correspondence between administrators (like me) and contractors (like you) to judge the relationship and to look for lapses in

4

professionalism or ethical conduct. This need not be a concern for you, but it might explain the rather direct nature of my correspondence as we proceed with this project.

The evaluator will be here in early June, so time is of the essence. For this reason I must be very clear with you about my intentions regarding the trees and my relationship with you. In short: **I need a proposal from you.**

If you'd prefer to give me a call and state your proposal over the phone, that would be acceptable, too. **Just give me a ring.**

Sincerely,

Walter

Walter Russ

P.S. I'm a little concerned about your friend Chef Angelo and his plans for our school lunch program. (See attached letter.)

31 March

To My New Friends in Geyser Creek:

Buon giorno! And thank you for the happy good hello to Geyser Creek. Our same friend, the *bella* Florence Waters, tells me how much I enjoy cooking for you. Already I know she is not making the mistake!

I am here in your town to take over the Geyser Creek Middle School cafeteria. But cooking for these young, small bellies is so easy for big important chef like me.

This is why I propose to you: Open the school cafeteria to everyone and I cook for all of Geyser Creek. We call it Caffè Angelo. Then all the people can enjoy the recipes that belong in my family for five generations. And your town's other little cafe? It can close.

So simple, yes?

Something else: It is custom in my country for chefs to live right near their *ristoranti*. I see a room on first floor of this school. Sign on the door says: MR. N.'S CLASSROOM. It is a small room, but not a problem. I will live there.

So simple, yes?

Scusi my English. I've not been in your country a long distance.

Ciao!

Chef Angelo

Chef Angelo
No. 1 Chef in the History of the World!

✶ THE GEYSER CREEK GAZETTE ✶
Our motto: "We have a nose for news!"

| Friday, April 1 | **Early Edition** | **50 cents** |

Caffè Angelo Opens in Middle School
"Imagine the *pastabilities*!" says Chef Angelo

With a tantalizing array of pastas, pizzas and calzones, Chef Angelo officially opened Caffè Angelo, formerly known as the Geyser Creek Middle School cafeteria.

"So it looks like school cafeteria now, yes?" Chef Angelo said yesterday at the grand opening. "But only imagine the *pastabilities*! In my mind I see red-and-white tablecloths. I see strolling musicians. I see pasta for everyone and everyone for pasta!"

Chef Angelo arrived in Geyser Creek one week ago to take over the school lunch program at Geyser Creek Middle School. He is a friend of Florence Waters.

For now Chef Angelo will live at the middle school.

"I am the easy guest," the Italian-born chef said. "I bring nothing with me except big love of good food and small trunk filled with my family's secret recipes passed down from the great-great-grandfather. He opens his first *ristorante* when he was only 16."

Angel Fisch, owner of Geyser Creek Cafe, was unimpressed.

Chef Angelo uses family recipes at Caffè Angelo.

"My recipes come from my great-great-great-aunt Starr," said Fisch. "She served the first Jell-O salad with marshmallows in town. And she was only 15."

Asked to respond to Chef Angelo's claim that he is the No. 1 chef in the history of the world, Fisch dished: "Well, that's *his* story."

Phone Tree Needed for Emergencies

Justin Case plants seed for phone tree.

Geyser Creek will soon have an emergency phone tree, thanks to Justin Case, Geyser Creek's new emergency director.

"A phone tree is a way to communicate emergency information to the community quickly and inexpensively," Case told the Geyser Creek City Council last night. "It's easy, too."

Case explained the process by which residents are assigned a name and phone number to call in times of emergency, disaster, or any suspicious activity that demands immediate action.

"If you get an answering machine, leave a message and keep calling down the list until you reach a live person," Case said. "When the person at the bottom of the phone tree calls the person at the top, we'll know the information has circulated throughout the community."

The Geyser Creek City Council approved adoption of the phone tree and asked Case to create and distribute the call list with instructions for a trial run.

Principal Russ Suggests Cutting Arbor Day Celebrations Short

Geyser Creek Middle School Principal Walter Russ asks that instead of planting trees this Arbor Day, local residents celebrate the holiday by trimming their trees.

"I see trees all over town that could use a good pruning," Russ told the Geyser Creek City Council last night. "I urge everyone to trim, rather than plant, the trees on their property."

Russ is especially eager to see the trees trimmed at Geyser Creek Middle School. He told the council he is soliciting bids for tree trimming and has asked designer Florence Waters to submit a proposal regarding the trees.

Waters, president of Flowing Waters Fountains, Etc., collaborated with Mr. Sam N.'s students at Geyser Creek Middle School to design the school's fountain and cafeteria sink.

Arbor Day is celebrated in Missouri on the first Friday of April. Traditionally, people *plant* trees rather than trim them.

"In this case it's important to branch out from the norm," Russ told council members. "Dangerous limbs create a safety hazard for children walking to and from school. Plus, they can be terribly unattractive. The limbs, I mean—not the children."

Walter Russ urges tree trimming.

Grand Opening

Caffè Angelo

Pasta! Pizza! Pomodori!

(formerly the Geyser Creek Middle School cafeteria)

Geyser Creek Cafe

All-AMERICAN Food

Fisch sticks

Biscuits

Fresh milk

No attitude

Angel Fisch, Owner

The Fountainhead Salon

Spring fever special

Cover your roots!

Introducing Tea-Tree Oil Root Treatment

Pearl O. Ster, Owner

Happy Arbor Day!

Don't be a stick in the mud.

Plant a tree!

GEYSER CREEK HISTORICAL SOCIETY

Now open to the public

Jeannie Ologee, Director
"We dig your roots!"

Letter to the Editor

Dear Editor:

As many of you know, I've spent the past year compiling historical records about our lovely town and the people who have been lucky enough to call it home.

If you'd like to research your family tree, or just want to read up on our town's fascinating history, please drop by.

Jeannie Ologee
Director, Geyser Creek Historical Society

Send your letters to: Annette Trap, Editor,
The Geyser Creek Gazette

Geyser Creek Barbershop

Fisher Cutbait, Barber

Haircuts Shaves No chitchat

PUBLIC NOTICE

Now accepting bids for a major tree-trimming and pruning project at Geyser Creek Middle School. Contact Principal Walter Russ for all inquiries regarding the trees.

No hurtful pranks, please.
But you may play a harmless joke on someone.

ANNOUNCEMENT: Please make Chef Angelo feel
welcome in our classroom. Imagine how uprooted he
must feel being so far from home.

TODAY'S ASSIGNMENT: Today is Arbor Day. Let's
research some interesting tree facts. We'll send our
findings to Florence.

Tree fact: A tree is a perennial* plant that usually has
a self-supporting trunk containing woody tissues.

***WORD OF THE DAY:** perennial. 1. that which
naturally renews its growth each year 2. occurring
again and again; everlasting

Italian lesson of the day:

English	Italian	Pronounced
yes/no	sì/no	see/no
okay	va bene	va be-neh
good day	buon giorno	bwon jor-no
hi/bye	ciao	chow
good-bye	arrivederci	ar-ree-ve-dare-chee

GEYSER CREEK MIDDLE SCHOOL
Geyser Creek, Missouri

April 1

Ms. Florence Waters
Our sixth-grade class's very best friend,
  who just happens to be the president of ...
Flowing Waters Fountains, Etc.
Watertown, California

Hi, Florence!

We're studying trees. Did you know two mature trees provide enough oxygen for a family of four? It's true!

Here's what else we've learned:

Trees are the largest and longest-living organisms on Earth. Some are even older than Mr. N.

Paddy

Throughout history every civilization has regarded trees with great respect.
Lily

Hospital patients heal faster and require shorter stays if their rooms face one or more trees. Our classroom faces lots of trees. These are the trees Wally wants you to trim.
Tad Poll

*The Italian word for <u>tree</u>
is <u>albero</u>. The Romans
believed the ancient god
Attis lent his spirit to the
pine tree, which became the
maypole.*
    Shelly

*The Celts planted trees in the names of their children to allow each
child's imagination to live in the earth and the wind. Isn't that
beautiful?   Minnie O.*

Trees are great for:
* climbing
* providing shade
* picnicking under
* decorating!

marshmallow

chocolate

caramel

cookie

I'd like to plant a picnic tree that grows all the treats
needed for a picnic.
                    Gil

Ragazza*

April 1

Gil and Tad:

Here's an idea for an April Fool's prank:

We write a note to Mr. N., inviting him to lunch today, and sign it from Goldie Fisch. You guys write a note to Goldie, inviting her to lunch with Mr. N., and sign *his* name. (We know they like each other, right?)

Harmless fun, *sì?*

Ciao!

Lily

Shelly   *Paddy*   Minnie O.

---

* *Ragazza* is Italian for *GIRL*.

14

RAGAZZO*

April 1

Shelly, Lily, Minnie O., and Paddy:

Si! Not only harmless. *Helpful.*

We'll deliver Goldie's note now.

Arrivederci!

Gil   Tad Poll

---

*Change the *A* to *O*, and you get the Italian word for *BOY*.

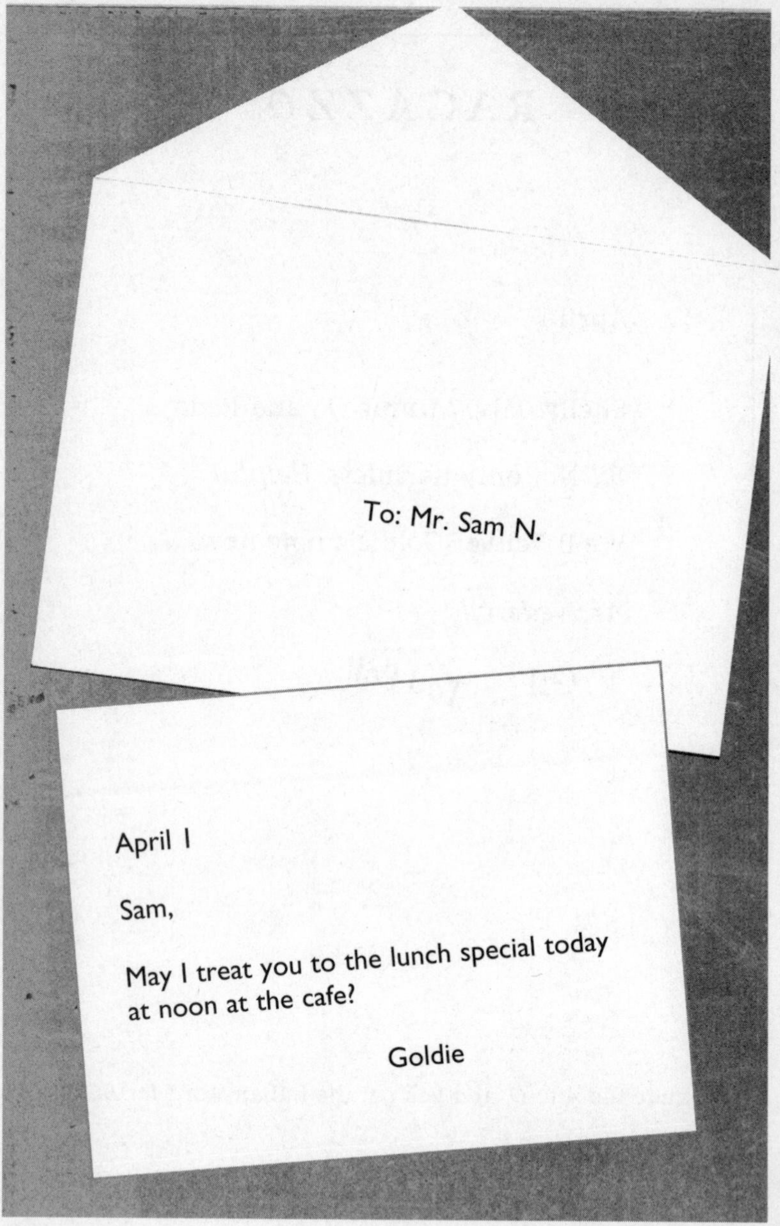
To: Mr. Sam N.

April 1

Sam,

May I treat you to the lunch special today at noon at the cafe?

Goldie

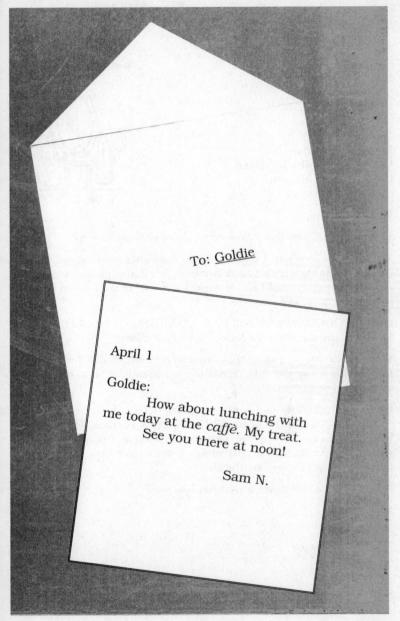

To: <u>Goldie</u>

April 1

Goldie:

　　How about lunching with
me today at the *caffè*. My treat.
See you there at noon!

　　　　Sam N.

17

'FLOWING WATERS FOUNTAINS, ETC.'

Watertown, California

April 2

Wally Russ
My Prince of a Pal
Geyser Creek Middle School
Geyser Creek, Missouri

Wally, listen.

I just received your letter. You want me to *propose* to you?

You know I adore you. I really do! And it touches me that you think our friendship has grown more serious. But, Wally, please. I *can't* give you a ring. It would never work. I suggest we keep our relationship purely professional.

OH FOR GOODNESS' SAKE! I AM LAUGHING OUT LOUD. I just looked at the date on your letter: April Fool's Day!

Well, forgive me for saying this, but I'm *relieved,* Wally. I would've felt terrible if you had misinterpreted our friendship as something more, you know, *romantico.*

Ha-ha! The joke's on me! Well, good. Now, let's talk about your trees. In fact, I *did* notice the beautiful trees on your campus. They're lovely! But I can see why you'd want to trim them. I don't use any special equipment for tree trimming—just things I have around the house or collect during my travels.

Do you have a hall tree? Would you like one?

Your *friend,*

Florence

P.S. Don't worry about Angelo. He'll do a *magnifico* job cooking for you and the students.

OVERNIGHT MAIL

April 4

Ms. Florence Waters
President
Flowing Waters Fountains, Etc.
Watertown, California

Dear Ms. Waters,

I don't know how to interpret your recent letter other than to say I couldn't be more serious about wanting a proposal from you. It's the only way I can engage you in the endeavor we both agree is necessary.

On the other hand, if you feel unqualified, please let me know. The students will be disappointed, of course, but I'll understand.

And no, I do not have a hall tree. Frankly, I'd like one to spruce up this office.

Please keep in mind that our correspondence will be reviewed by an evaluator from the Society of Principals and Administrators. Any indication of graft and/or corruption would be the end of my career and likely yours, too.

I'm told that my evaluator will be Leif Blite, who is known in education circles as the Velvet Ax. Mr. Blite is scheduled to visit in June, so time is obviously an issue here.

Speaking of time, your friend Chef Angelo insists that a child should not be expected to eat lunch in less than three hours, after which a two-hour *siesta* must be taken. I hope you can appreciate my concern.

Sincerely,

Walter

Walter Russ

Watertown, California

April 5

Wally Russ
Princey PAL
Geyser Creek Middle School
Geyser Creek, Missouri

Dear Wally,

So you *were* serious about wanting a proposal from me? Oh
dear. This is awkward. But, Wally, only you would refer to an
engagement as an "endeavor we both agree is necessary."

No, it's not necessary. But if it *were*, a proposal from *me* isn't
the only way to get engaged. *YOU* could propose, you know.

Here's the thing: I don't want you to. Really, I don't. I want to
be your pal and I want to trim the school trees. Okay?

But, Wally, I *do* love your idea of a spruce for a hall tree! Dare
I go out on a limb and say you're really starting to grow on
me?

Gotta run. Lots to do! The sixth graders sent me some *treemendous* ideas!

Mwaa, mwaa, as the Italians say when they kiss a *friend's*
cheeks.

Florence

P.S. What kind of nickname is Velvet Ax? Is it because
Mr. Blite is such a sharp dresser?

20

P.P.S. I *do* appreciate your concern about Angelo. I need at *least* two and a half hours for my *siestas*. I'll speak to Angelo about this when I'm in town to trim the trees.

P.P.P.S. Wally, I put the *sì* in *siestas!*

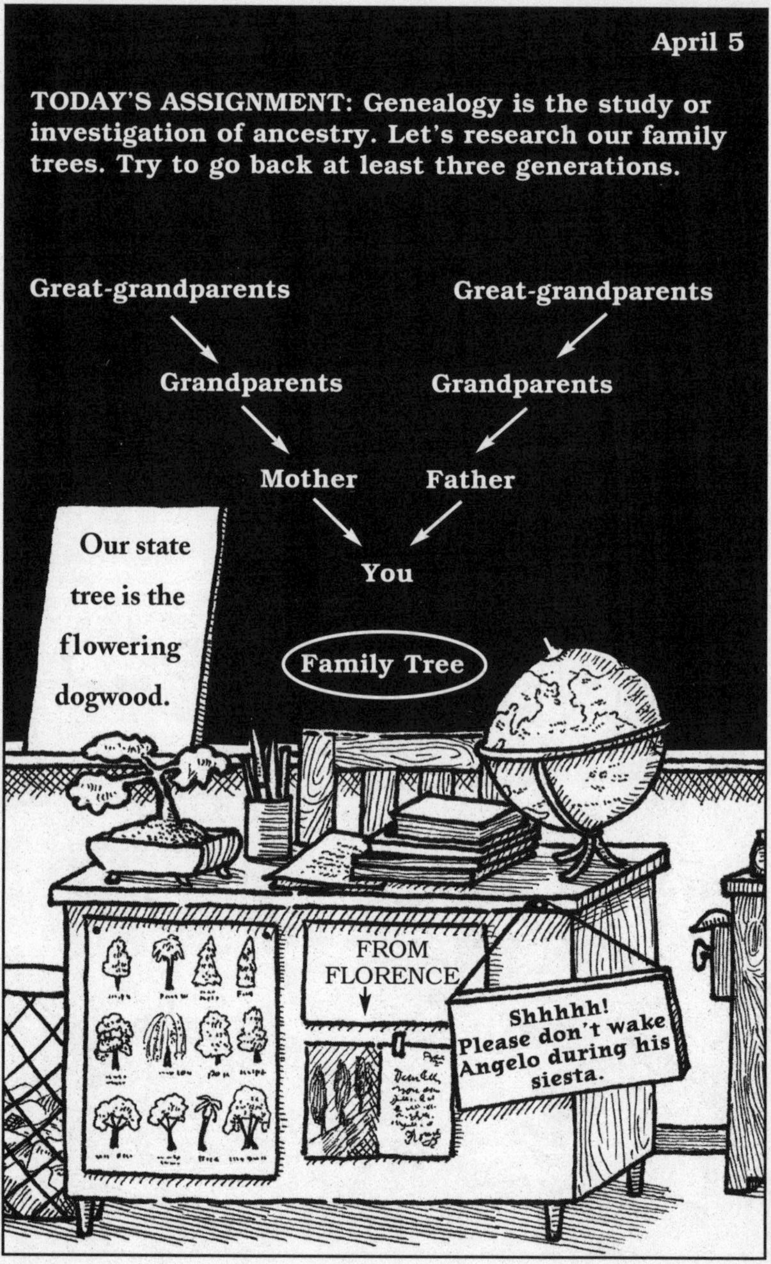
April 5
TODAY'S ASSIGNMENT: Genealogy is the study or investigation of ancestry. Let's research our family trees. Try to go back at least three generations.
Great-grandparents
Great-grandparents
Grandparents
Grandparents
Mother
Father
You
Our state tree is the flowering dogwood.
Family Tree
FROM FLORENCE
Shhhhh! Please don't wake Angelo during his siesta.

Italian lesson of the day:

English	Italian	Pronounced
please	per favore	pair fa-vor-eh
thank you	grazie	gra-zyeh
sorry/excuse me	mi scusi	mee skoo-zee
family	famiglia	fa-meal-ya
to snore	russare	roossah-reh

April 5

Mr. N.,

Please don't make me research my _famiglia_ tree. I don't have one. My mom adopted me when I was a baby. She's never told me anything more than that, and I can't bring myself to ask her where I came from—or why I have such a strange name.

But I can't make a family tree out of just my mom and me. It would look more like a twig.

My mom

Me

I hope you'll keep my secret and not tell the whole class. _Per favore_?

Minnie O.

P.S. I think it was quite mean of you to break your lunch date with Goldie Fisch. _Mi scusi_, but that's just my opinion.

GEYSER CREEK MIDDLE SCHOOL
Geyser Creek, Missouri

Sam N.
Sixth-Grade Teacher

April 5

Minnie O.,

Of course I understand.

Instead of researching your family tree, please prepare a report on the history of the trees on our
school campus.

Thanks for confiding in me. I know it's hard to tell
someone a personal secret. It's sometimes even
harder to keep one. But don't worry. Your secret is
safe with me. That's what friends are for.

Speaking of friendships, please don't concern yourself with my personal life or Goldie's. Some things
aren't meant to be. In my case, a simple friendship
with Goldie Fisch is one of them.

Grazie.

Mr. N.

Jeannie Ologee, Director

April 6

Minnie O.
c/o Mr. N.'s Sixth-Grade Class
Geyser Creek Middle School
Geyser Creek, Missouri

Dear Minnie O.,

Thanks for visiting the Geyser Creek Historical Society yesterday afternoon. I hope you enjoyed the tour.

I'm sorry I wasn't able to provide much information regarding the trees at the middle school. After you left I thought of something that might be helpful in your research: the Maids of May.

Have you ever heard of them? I bet not. Long ago the Maids of May were a secret society of single women who spent their time—and considerable fortunes—planting trees all over the world, including here in Spring Creek, as our town was called back then. (Of course, you know all about the history of our town after the research project regarding the fountain you and your classmates conducted last year!)

The Maids of May held only one official meeting each year—at one minute after midnight on the first day of May. I'm sending along their minutes for you to read. I haven't had a chance to read them myself, but I did notice that the Maids didn't date their entries. You'll have to use other sources to determine just when these meetings took place.

I can tell you how old the first entry is—75 years old—because my granny Zoe and grandpa Gene will celebrate their 75th wedding anniversary in June.

Good luck with your research project!

Historically yours,

Jeannie Ologee

Jeannie Ologee

MINUTES FROM THE MEETING OF THE MAIDS OF MAY

Twenty-seven members attended the annual meeting, which began with the composition and recitation of verses 51 and 52 of our pledge:

We are the Maids of May—
And this is the song we sing
When we meet each year to celebrate
Our lives, our dreams, and spring.

We are the Maids of May—
Our goal, please comprehend,
Is to sow the seeds of happiness
By planting trees with friends.

Thereafter, Maids approved the minutes from our previous meeting. Members then discussed our recent trip to Thailand, where we visited the night market and camped with the hill tribe people. We also studied the local vegetation and helped villagers plant 1,000 teak trees.

Elm Blite   Starr Fisch

Here we are in Thailand!

Closer to home, Maids spent much of the year putting the finishing touches on the Spring Creek Public Library. Thanks to Colette for overseeing the construction!

At long last—a library!

Turning to new business, Maids resumed discussion of our plan to ask local schoolchildren to help us plant saplings along Spring Creek. The area is currently occupied by one tree, the gracious weeping willow planted by our founding mothers 25 years ago at the first meeting of the Maids of May. Maid Elm Blite suggested we pay students a silver dollar for every sapling they plant. Good idea, Elm!

Zoe Keenie will depart our sorority next month when she marries Gene Ologee. Best wishes, Zoe!

We concluded our meeting with refreshments (ladyfingers and ginger tea) prepared by me (Starr Fisch), followed by a celebratory dance around the weeping willow. Zoe snapped a photograph of us.

Respectfully submitted,

Starr Fisch

Starr Fisch
Secretary, Maids of May

Maids celebrate May Day with song and dance.

⋆THE GEYSER CREEK GAZETTE⋆

Our motto: "We have a nose for news!"

| Thursday, April 7 | Late Edition | 50 cents |

Recipe for Disaster
Battle heats up between *caffè* and cafe

Chef Angelo calls Angel's pasta *"al musho."*

Well, it *seemed* like a good idea.

Restaurateurs Angel Fisch and Chef Angelo agreed to prepare lunch for each other yesterday in an attempt to establish peace.

Fisch, owner of Geyser Creek Cafe, sent a plate of her famous macaroni and cheese to Chef Angelo, who now heads up the Geyser Creek Middle School lunch program. In return he prepared and delivered a bowl of *penne ai quattro formaggi* (pasta with four cheeses), a recipe passed down from his great-great-grandfather.

It was a recipe for disaster.

"What this woman does to pasta is the abomination," Chef Angelo said after tasting Fisch's macaroni. "Pasta should be cooked *al*

Angel Fisch proposes devilish cook-off.

dente—with a little good resistance to the teeth. This is *al musho.*"

After describing Chef Angelo's pasta as "all macho," Fisch challenged Chef Angelo to a cook-off.

"I say we let the good folks in this town decide who's the better cook," said Fisch.

Chef Angelo accepted the challenge. "The best chef, may he win," he said.

"And may the worst chef lose his *caffè*," hissed Fisch, who agreed to let Chef Angelo pick the time and place for the culinary showdown.

"I can beat that man like egg whites anytime, anywhere," she said.

Cook-off Expected to Divide Town Loyalties

Locals are divided over where to eat lunch.

News of the cook-off between Angel Fisch and Chef Angelo received mixed reactions from locals, who are already choosing sides between Geyser Creek's homegrown cook and the Italian chef.

"This is complicated," said Sam N., sixth-grade teacher at Geyser Creek Middle School. "Chef Angelo is new in town and it's important to make him feel welcome. That's why I've been eating most of my meals at Caffè Angelo."

Goldie Fisch, secretary at the middle school, disagrees.

"I think it's important to support our hometown businesses," said Fisch. "Besides, Angel is my sister, and I refuse to eat food prepared by a man who would insult my sister or her cooking."

Pearl O. Ster, owner of The Fountainhead

(Continued on page 2, column 2)

Principal Waiting for Proposal and Ring from Waters

Principal Russ says weeping willow tree is dangerous.

The tree-trimming project at Geyser Creek Middle School is still on, Principal Walter Russ told the Geyser Creek School Board last night.

"I'm just waiting for a proposal from Florence Waters," Russ said.

Russ told the board that in addition to being trimmed, some trees on the school campus will require more drastic measures.

"The weeping willow tree behind the school should be eliminated," said Russ, who outlined the safety hazards associated with the 60-foot tree.

Principal Russ will be evaluated in June by Leif Blite, branch chief for the Society of Principals and Administrators. The landscaping of the school campus is one of several categories Blite will evaluate at the middle school.

Because of cutbacks in funding for education, Geyser Creek Middle School has not been evaluated in two years. Asked if he's concerned about Blite's reaction to the school's unique fountain and sink, as well as its unusual relationship with designer Florence Waters, Russ said: "My relationship with Florence Waters is serious, which is why I have recently asked her to give me a proposal and a ring. Mr. Blite should have no objections."

COOK-OFF *(Continued from page 1, column 2)*

Salon, expressed the middle ground.

"This is a real doozy, folks," Ster said. "Angel is my friend and customer, but I agree it's important to make newcomers feel welcome. That's why I've been alternating between the cafe and the *caffè*. Angel and Angelo are both good cooks, and they've both got pretty good hair. But I'm going to give Angelo a coupon for a tea-tree oil conditioning treatment. He could use it."

Phone Tree Cut Short by Personality

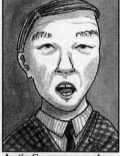

Geyser Creek's new phone tree must be rebuilt from the ground up, says emergency director Justin Case.

"During our trial run yesterday, we discovered some personality conflicts that

Justin Case says new phone tree must be built.

resulted in a breakdown in communications," said Case.

Though Case refused to identify the root of the conflict, an unnamed source said the breakdown occurred when Goldie Fisch, secretary at Geyser Creek Middle School, refused to call sixth-grade teacher Sam N. The same source (okay, it was Pearl O. Ster) said she asked Goldie if she couldn't put aside her personality conflict with Sam N. for the purpose of the phone tree.

"I said, 'Honey, if there's an emergency, couldn't you call Sam?'" Ster said. "Goldie said she *especially* wouldn't call him if there's an emergency. Hoo-ee. And I thought those two were sorta sweet on each other. Oh well."

Case assured residents that a revised phone tree would be sent out soon and a trial run rescheduled.

Caffè Angelo

Now serving:

Linguine with Angelo's Mussels

Letter to the Editor

Dear Editor:

    Hi! I'm writing to encourage everyone to visit the new Geyser Creek Historical Society. It's a fascinating place filled with documents that trace the story of our town's past. Until I visited, I never knew what an important role women played in the history of our town. Maybe a better name for our new historical society would be the Geyser Creek *Her*storical Society.

Respectfully submitted,

Minnie O.
Sixth-Grade Student, GCMS

Letters to the editor are always welcome.
Send them to: Annette Trap, Editor,
The Geyser Creek Gazette

Geyser Creek Cafe

Early Fisch Special

New!

The Angelo Omelet
Ham • Cheese • And mostly baloney

Angel Fisch, Owner

The Fountainhead Salon

Cover those roots!

Special Tea-Tree Oil Root Treatment

Organic   Nontoxic   Safe   Natural

Pearl O. Ster, Owner

April 7

Hey, Shelly.

I still think it's lousy the way Goldie stood
Mr. N. up for lunch on April Fool's Day. I
asked Mr. N. about it. He told me Goldie
never showed up at Caffè Angelo.

At least the new cafeteria food is good—
especially the pizza. Isn't Angelo the best
chef ever?

Gil

April 7

Gil!

<u>The way Goldie stood Mr. N. up?</u> Mr. N.'s the one who didn't show. Angel says she kept a lunch special warm for him till two o'clock, but he never came by the café.

Not that it matters. Why in the world would Goldie want to have lunch with someone who supports Chef Angelo after all the hateful things he said about Angel?

Mr. N. just doesn't get it. And apparently neither do you.

Shelly

P.S. For your information, the Italians didn't even invent pizza. The Babylonians, Israelites, Egyptians, and other ancient Middle Eastern cultures were eating flat unleavened bread cooked in mud ovens long before the Italians <u>stole</u> the idea.

April 7

Shelly:

Angelo had it right. Women: *Aye-yi-yi.*

Gil

Ragazza

April 7

Angel Fisch
Geyser Creek Cafe
On the Square
Geyser Creek, Missouri

HAND DELIVERED

Dear Angel,

We just wanted to let you know that we're behind
you 100 percent.

We all got permission from our parents to order lunch
from your cafe so we can support you and *not* Chef
Angelo. It'll be a total *boy*cott.

Your friends and fans,

Lily

Paddy   *Shelly*

P.S. I'm starting a girls-only club. Do you want to
join? Meetings are held once a year on May 1.
There's one club rule: You can't get married, which is
pretty easy, considering the boys in Geyser Creek.

Minnie O.

Geyser Creek Cafe

Where Angel's Food Is Heavenly

On the Square   Geyser Creek, Missouri

Angel Fisch,
Cook and Owner

April 7

Dear Lily, Paddy, Minnie O., and Shelly,

Thanks, girls. I really appreciate it. I'll be happy to deliver lunch to you at school. It'll also give me a chance to spy on the enemy: Chef Angelo!

And about that girls-only club? I'm in!

xo Angel

RAGAZZO

April 7

Chef Angelo:

We think it's really crummy how the girls in our class are *boy*cotting Caffè Angelo. If it makes you feel any better, they're not talking to us, either.

If you need help in the *caffè*, just let us know. We guys need to stick together, since we're sorta outnumbered here.

Anyway, we really like your cooking.

Tad Poll   Gil

Chef Angelo

7 April

Dear the Tad Poll with the Gil,

Such good boys are you to help make Caffè Angelo the number one *ristorante* in Geyser Creek!

You will like to be musicians in my *caffè*? Stroll around. Play music for guests! I bring a violin and an accordion with me in trunk. You will have these.

Good-bye for right now. I have a hair meeting with the Pearl.

Chef Angelo

Chef Angelo
No. 1 Chef in the History of the World!

Geyser Creek Middle School
Geyser Creek, Missouri

April 8

EXPRESS MAIL

Florence Waters
Founder and President
Flowing Waters Fountains, Etc.
Watertown, California

Dear Florence,

Hi! Have you ever had a <u>girled</u> cheese sandwich? I hadn't until today, when Angel Fisch delivered lunch to all the girls in our class.

Guess what? I'm researching the trees on our school campus. Jeannie Ologee at the Geyser Creek Historical Society dug out an old book for me. It has all the notes from meetings held by a group of ladies called the Maids of May.

You can read for yourself about the Maids. I'll send you copies of the minutes as I go through them. It's a little confusing because the minutes aren't dated, so I have to figure out when they were written. It's not as hard as it sounds. The minutes I'm sending were written the year after the first entry I read, which Ms. Ologee told me was 75 years old.

So far I've discovered that the huge weeping willow tree at our school was planted by the Maids 100 years ago. I think it's terrible that Principal Russ wants to cut it down. What can we do?

Love,
Minnie O.

MINUTES FROM THE MEETING OF THE MAIDS OF MAY

Twenty-two members attended our May meeting, which began with the composition and recitation of verses 53 and 54 of the Maids Pledge:

We are the Maids of May—
Who meet each year in secrecy,
Not for evil purposes.
Nor to practice witchery.

If you say to a Maid of May,
"Please tell me your philosophy,"
Her answer will likely be:
"I just want to leave a legacy."

After hearing and approving the minutes from our previous meeting, the Maids discussed old business, including our recent trip to Egypt, where we studied the Phoenician juniper and planted 200 eucalyptus trees. We also made time for a quick cruise down the Nile.

Queens of the Nile!

Therein followed a discussion of the successful tree-planting festival we sponsored earlier this year. Elm Blite reported that more than 225 walnut trees were planted by a class of sixth-grade students from Spring Creek School. As promised, the Maids paid the children a silver dollar per sapling. Attached for our records is a photo of the project and a thank-you note from the class. It's worth noting that Wilhomena Furr is the daughter of Olive Branch, who was a Maid before she married Douglas Furr.

In other news, we lost four members this year. Sadie got scarlet fever and had to move to Springfield for medical care. Beatrice, Vanessa, and Clarissa got married. Best of luck, girls!

Business matters behind us, we then turned our attention to our annual reception, which featured an array of delectable finger foods, gracefully prepared by our star chef, Starr Fisch.

Respectfully submitted,

Maggie Nolya

Maggie Nolya
Secretary, Maids of May

Dear Maids of May:

We send sincere thanks for letting our class help plant the walnut trees along the banks of Spring Creek. It will be fun to watch the trees grow up with us!

Thanks, too, for the $225. We spent twenty dollars for our sixth-grade class tea. We're saving the rest for our high school graduation cotillion.

Kind regards,

Wilhomena Furr

Wilhomena Furr
Class Secretary
The Sixth-Grade Class of Spring Creek School

ʹF̲LOWING W̲ATERS F̲OUNTAINS, E̲TC.ʹ

Watertown, California

OVERNIGHT EXPRESS

April 11

Minnie O.
c/o Mr. N.'s Sixth-Grade Class
Geyser Creek Middle School
Geyser Creek, Missouri

Dear Minnie O.,

Thanks for the terrific research! This is so helpful because to trim a tree properly, you must understand its roots. They're like a tree's secret history.

You don't mean that Wally wants to cut down the weeping willow, do you? I thought he wanted me to *trim* it—and all the trees on your school campus.

Don't worry, sweets. I'll handle Wally if you'll keep sending me any information you dig up regarding the trees.

Also, would you measure the hall outside Wally's office and ask him what kind of wood he'd like for his hall tree? Do you think Goldie Fisch would like her own hall tree?

Your friend,

Florence

P.S. I don't have Angel Fisch's address at the cafe. Could you please see that the box I'm sending along is delivered to her? It'll be perfect for her new delivery service, don't you think? Just make sure she wears a helmet!

Date Set for Cook-off: May 1

Chef Angelo and Angel Fisch agree on date for cook-off.

The cook-off between Chef Angelo and Angel Fisch will be Sunday, May 1.

"May Day is always the big happy day of the year in Italy," Chef Angelo said. "So that is the day we have our cook-off. After that the lady cook can close the other cafe in town. I don't remember her name."

Fisch, owner of Geyser Creek Cafe, proposed the idea for the culinary showdown. She left the date and time of the event to Chef Angelo.

"May 1 is fine by me," Fisch said. "If that pompous pasta-for-brains thinks he can top my great-great-great-aunt Starr's recipe for macaroni and cheese, he better wake up and smell the burnt toast."

Chef Angelo will prepare his great-great-grandfather's recipe for *penne ai quattro formaggi*, or pasta with four cheeses.

"It is so simple to any person that I will be the No. 1 winner of cook-off," Chef Angelo announced yesterday as he served lunch at Caffè Angelo.

"In your dreams, garlic breath!" Fisch quipped as she zipped through the cafeteria on her new Italian scooter.

Root Damage

Chef Angelo says his roots were damaged at The Fountainhead Salon.

Chef Angelo was told the special tea-tree oil treatment would condition his scalp. Instead, it damaged his roots.

So claims the Italian chef.

"The Pearl, she give me 20 percent-off coupon," Angelo said. "Then she ruin my hair. See how unhappy my roots they are now?"

Pearl O. Ster, owner of The Fountainhead Salon, denied all responsibility for the alleged

(Continued on page 2, column 2)

Geyser Creek Cafe

Now Delivering   **Girls-Only Lunches**

Go Fisch!

GO FISCH!

New! Angelo's-a-Chicken-Fried Steak

Angel Fisch, Owner

Sixth Grader Says: "Leaf the Trees Alone!"

Minnie O. makes leaflets to rake in support for school trees.

Geyser Creek Middle School sixth grader Minnie O. has launched "Leaf the Trees Alone," a campaign to save the trees on the school campus.

Minnie O. said that by leafleting local homes and businesses, she hopes to raise awareness of both the trees' history and of the people who planted them.

"I've been researching the trees on our school campus," said Minnie O. "It's a fascinating account of people who wanted to leave us something to remember them by."

Minnie O., 11, the daughter of Dr. Sandy Beech, says the giant weeping willow tree behind the school was planted 100 years ago by the Maids of May, an all-female organization dedicated to planting trees around the world.

According to Minnie O., the Maids paid schoolchildren to plant the saplings that have grown into the walnut grove behind the middle school.

"The Maids were so cool," said Minnie O. "They didn't need boys to have fun. I'm starting a new chapter of the Maids of May for all the single girls in Geyser Creek."

The Maids of May consisted of unmarried women.

"Sororities for single women were not uncommon in earlier years," said Jeannie Ologee, director of the Geyser Creek (Name to Be Announced) Society.

ROOT *(Continued from page 1, column 1)*
root damage.

"It's his own dadjing fault," Ster stated. "I asked him before we started if he dyes his hair. He said no. So I used the regular formula treatment, which unfortunately accentuated his gray roots. If he'd been honest and told me he dyes his hair, I would've used the treatment for permed and color-treated hair."

Angelo said he had already been in contact with barber Fisher Cutbait.

"Never again will I step the foot in the Pearl's salon," Chef Angelo said. "Only a man can repair this tragedy."

"Fine," said Ster. "See if I ever eat in your ding-dang *caffè* again."

Letter to the Editor

Dear Editor:

On behalf of the men and boys in this town, I'm writing in response to Minnie O.'s recent letter in which she suggested replacing the word Historical with *Her*storical at the new Geyser Creek Historical Society.

We support the name change wholeheartedly, given the very important role women played in the history of our town.

In exchange we ask only that the women and girls acknowledge the important role *men* have played and continue to play. To this end we propose changing the spelling of Geyser Creek to Guys "R" Creek.

Sincerely,

Gil
Sixth-Grade Student
Guys "R" Creek Middle School

Although letters to the editor are always welcome, some letters are more welcome than others.
Send yours to: Annette Trap, Editor,
The Geyser Creek Gazette

By Special Proclamation
of Guys "R" Creek
Mayor T. B. Newt
April is:
It's Good to Be a Guy Month
in
Guys "R" Creek, Missouri

Parking tickets waived for men.

The Fountainhead Salon

Pearl's Tea-Tree Oil Root Treatment

**Some people might lie,
but your roots never will.**

Pearl O. Ster, Owner

**FREE ADS in the *Gazette*
for Women-Owned Businesses!**
Compliments of Annette Trap, Editor

Caffè Angelo

Speciali del giorno:

also dyes her
Angel-Hair Pasta

Chef Angelo

LEAF THE TREES ALONE!
Have you received your free copy of
"Herstory of Our Trees"?
If not, please contact Minnie O.

The Fountainhead Salon

Where Every Day Is a Good Hair Day

104 Main Street
Geyser Creek, Missouri

April 13

Miss Minnie O.
c/o Mr. N.'s Sixth-Grade Class
Geyser Creek Middle School
Geyser Creek, Missouri

Honey,

Can I join that all-gal group of yours? I've had it up to <u>here</u> with men and their egos.

I'll bring my curling wand to the meeting. Updos for everyone!

Yours in the sisterhood,

Pearl

LEAF THE TREES ALONE

Minnie O., Founder and President

April 14

Pearl O. Ster
Owner, The Fountainhead Salon
104 Main Street
Geyser Creek, Missouri

Dear Pearl,

Sure!

We're meeting at one minute after midnight on May 1, under the giant weeping willow tree—if Wally hasn't chopped it down!

Sincerely,

Minnie O.

47

LEAF THE TREES ALONE

MINNIE O., FOUNDER AND PRESIDENT

April 14

Hi, Goldie!

Florence asked if I thought you'd like a hall tree of your own. Would you?

Also, I want to tell you that I'm really sorry about Mr. N. and you. But after the way he stood you up for lunch, I think you're better off without him.

I'm starting a Maids of May club. Do you want to join? You just have to come to a meeting on May 1 at one minute after midnight. Oh, and you also have to <u>not</u> get married—ever.

Sincerely,

Minnie O.

48

From the Desk of Goldie Fisch

April 14

Minnie O.:

Isn't it just like Florence to ask if I'd like my own hall tree? Truth is, I can use Wally's. I really just need a place to hang my sweater. I'll tell Florence myself. I'm working on a letter to her right now.

Please don't worry about Mr. N. and me. I'll tell you a secret if you promise not to tell anyone: I used to have a harmless little crush on him.

NOT anymore!

I'd love to join the Maids of May! See you at the meeting. I'll bring a ...big surprise!

Goldie

Goldie Fisch
Geyser Creek Middle School
Geyser Creek, Missouri

URGENT

CONFIDENTIAL

Ms. Florence Waters
Friend, Adviser, and Confidante
c/o Flowing Waters Fountains, Etc.
Watertown, California

Geyser Creek
MO
14
APRIL
A.M.

Sadie
Hawkins

USA

OPEN IMMEDIATELY!

SOCIETY OF PRINCIPALS AND ADMINISTRATORS

Making the World Safe for Bureaucracy

10 Maple Leaf Plaza

April 14

OVERNIGHT EXPRESS

Mr. Walter Russ
Principal
Geyser Creek Middle School
Geyser Creek, Missouri

Mr. Russ:

This letter is to inform you that your evaluation will be on May 1 rather than in June, as previously scheduled.

Thank you.

Bureaucratically yours,

Leif Blite

Leif Blite
Branch Chief, Evaluators of Lower Midwest (ELM)

GEYSER CREEK MIDDLE SCHOOL
Geyser Creek, Missouri
Our NEW school motto: *Go with the Flo!*

Mr. Walter Russ
Principal

FAX

DATE: April 15
TO: Leif Blite
FR: Walter Russ
RE: My evaluation

Mr. Blite,

I must say that I find it unfair to move up my evaluation by an entire month.

We've experienced some unusual complications this year regarding (of all things!) a cafeteria sink. Last year we had some issues regarding a leaky drinking fountain. And now the trees on our school campus are in dire need of trimming. I'd like to get that taken care of before you arrive to evaluate me.

In addition, May 1 is a Sunday, and I generally do not work on weekends. Will you please consider rescheduling your visit for sometime in June?

Thank you for understanding.

Professionally yours,

Walter Russ

Walter Russ

P.S. The director of our new historical society tells me we have a Blite in our town records. A relative of yours, perhaps? I'd be happy to do some genealogical research for you, if you're interested.

SOCIETY OF PRINCIPALS AND ADMINISTRATORS

Making the World Safe for Bureaucracy

10 Maple Leaf Plaza   Washington, D.C.

FACSIMILE

DATE: April 15
TO: Walter Russ
FR: Leif Blite
RE: Your evaluation

Principal Russ:

In fact, I *have* heard of your school's sink and fountain. Why do you think I moved up the date for your evaluation?

I have also received information that the contractor who designed your school's deviant fountain and cafeteria sink has sent peacocks, swans, flamingos, monkeys, build-your-own-beach kits, and other assorted *novelties* to the students at your school.

Until you mentioned it, I hadn't heard anything regarding the trees on your school campus. But I now have cause for concern on that front as well.

You think it's unfair of me to move up the date of your evaluation by an entire month? Principal Russ, *all's* fair in love and school administration.

See you on May 1.

Bureaucratically yours,

Leif Blite

Leif Blite
Branch Chief, Evaluators of Lower Midwest (ELM)

P.S. My father's great-aunt Elm was a spinster who lived somewhere in Missouri, perhaps in your village. Please don't trouble yourself researching my family tree. Genealogy holds little interest for me; old maids even less.

OVERNIGHT MAIL

April 15

Ms. Florence Waters
President
Flowing Waters Fountains, Etc.
Watertown, California

RE: THE TREES

Dear Ms. Waters,

Once again, as is becoming our habit, I fear we have gotten off on the wrong foot. And because time is now the enemy, I must be as blunt as possible.

Do you have any experience working in or for a nursery? If you don't, I'm not sure you are the right person for the task at hand. And if that's the case, I must continue my search for a more suitable partner for this endeavor.

Please let me know **A S A P.**

Keep in mind, too, that my relationship with you will be judged by Mr. Leif Blite from the Society of Principals and Administrators. Mr. Blite will likely read *all* of our correspondence when he conducts my evaluation on May 1—not in June, as previously indicated.

(And if I can address Mr. Blite directly here, let me say, sir, that although I have never met you, I'm sure your nickname, the Velvet Ax, is wholly undeserved of a fine, fair, reasonable gentleman like you.)

If it's not too much trouble, Ms. Waters, I would still like a hall tree, please. You may bill me personally for it.

Ethically,

Walter

Walter Russ

54

Watertown, California

April 16

Wally Russ
The Wally-Nut Principal
Geyser Creek Middle School
Geyser Creek, Missouri

Oh, Wally.

So this is how it's going to be, is it? Asking me if I have experience in a nursery?

Would it interest you to know that some of my best friends are babies? Or that I have a nursery in my own home? But Wally, please, how many times do I have to tell you? *I am not interested in proposals, rings, or having children with you.*

Let me be as blunt as I can be: I think you *should* continue your search if a proposal is what you're after. And if you want to know A SAP, I'm afraid I can't help you. I'll admit I have a weakness for sentimental movies, but I am *not* a sap. (Sorry.)

Now, if I may address Mr. Blite directly: Sir, it's bad enough that you read other people's mail. But to evaluate letter writers on their marital status? I mean, really. I've been single my entire life, and if you think it's held me back one iota, you're nuttier than Wally's walnut trees.

I wonder, Mr. Blite, if you were given your Velvet Ax nickname because you're not sharp at all but a bit dull? Hmmmmmmm. Maybe? Don't worry! This is very common with administrative types. We can work on it. You should've seen Wally before I met him. (Right, Wally?)

But, boys, no time to chat. I've got to get a move on if I'm going to trim more than a hundred trees by May 1.

Your singular sensation,

Flo

55

LEAF THE TREES ALONE

OUR MISSION: TO SAVE THE TREES AT GEYSER CREEK MIDDLE SCHOOL

MINNIE O., FOUNDER AND PRESIDENT

April 16

Florence Waters
Friend of the Trees
Flowing Waters Fountains, Etc.
Watertown, California

Dear Florence:

The measurements of the hall outside Wally's office are:

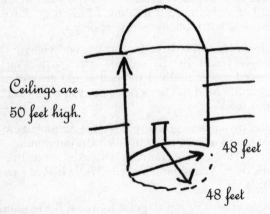

Ceilings are
50 feet high.

48 feet

48 feet

Wally says he doesn't care what kind of wood you use for the hall tree. He just wants a place to hang up his coat and hat. But he did tell me to tell you that he likes maple, walnut, mahogany, and pine.

I asked Wally if he was serious about cutting down the weeping willow tree. Guess what he said— "Either it goes or I go." Goldie says he's worried he'll flunk his evaluation from the Society of Principals and Administrators because the trees on campus are a safety hazard.

So I've launched a campaign to save the trees. When people know the true story of the trees at our school, maybe they'll be interested in protecting them.

I've still got lots of research to do. I'm enclosing the next section in the Maids of May minutes, where they discuss the trees. I could tell this entry was written 68 years ago because the students who planted the trees are now seniors in high school—or six years older than in the last entry I sent you.

Love,
    Minnie O.

MINUTES FROM THE MEETING OF THE MAIDS OF MAY

Fourteen members attended the May meeting, which began with the composition and recitation of verses 65 and 66 of the Maids Pledge:

> We are the Maids of May.
> We're part of a sorority
> That honors all of nature—
> Especially the art of botany!
>
> We are the Maids of May.
> We are that rarity
> Who ask nothing more of life than
> To live organically.

After reading and approving the minutes from our last meeting, we discussed old business, including our recent trip to Tuscany, where we studied the native olive trees and planted 200 Missouri dogwoods before skinny-dipping our way up the Amalfi coast.

Maid you look!

So long to members Martha, Emily, and Sarah, who all married this year. Best wishes, ladies!

Respectfully submitted,

Elm Blite

Elm Blite
Secretary and Skinny-dipper

P.S. Remember the children who planted the walnut saplings with us along the banks of Spring Creek? With the money we paid them, they held their Senior Cotillion under the Maids' weeping willow. Attached for our records is a photograph from the students.

Thanks to the Maids of May for making our Senior Cotillion a great success!

Wilhomena Furr,
Senior Class President

This is my date! His name is Will U. Merrame. Isn't he handsome?

⋆THE GEYSER CREEK GAZETTE⋆
Our motto: "We have a nose for news!"

| Sunday, April 17 | **Early Edition** | 50 cents |

Principal Urges Ratcheting and Hatcheting;
Sixth-grader says, "Ax not!"

Bad.

More like: *Badbadbadbadbad.*

That's how Geyser Creek Middle School Principal Walter Russ described the news that Leif Blite, branch chief of the Society of Principals and Administrators, will be in town on May 1 to review Russ's administrative skills.

Known as the Velvet Ax, Blite is famous for his smooth but brutal style, and because he presents a golden ax to principals who fail their evaluations. Blite was originally scheduled to visit in June. He will grade Russ in various categories, including maintenance of the middle school campus.

"What this means is that we have to ratchet up our efforts to hatchet down some of the unsightly and dangerous trees on campus," Russ told the *Gazette*. "There's no time for trimming and pruning. Clear-cutting is the only way to clean up this place."

According to Russ, the giant weeping willow tree behind the school should get the ax first.

"Not only is the tree a hazard, a weeping willow presents morale issues for a school," said Russ. "Frankly, I find it depressing."

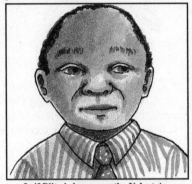

Leif Blite is known as the Velvet Ax.

Meanwhile, budding tree advocate Minnie O., a sixth-grade student at Geyser Creek Middle School, said she remains committed to saving the trees.

"The trees on our school campus are a living legacy to people who cared deeply about this community and its future," Minnie O. said in a press conference held yesterday under the weeping willow. "Ax not! It's what you can do for your country and for your town."

Phone Tree Needs New Trunk

Justin Case agrees to revise phone tree.

It happened again.

The second trial run of Geyser Creek's new emergency phone tree failed when one resident refused to call the person assigned to him. This time it's no mystery where the knot in the phone tree occurred.

Sam N., sixth-grade teacher at Geyser Creek Middle School, told the *Gazette:* "I'm very sorry, but I'm not comfortable calling Goldie Fisch for the phone tree. Justin Case will just have to create a different calling order."

Case, Geyser Creek's emergency director, agreed to devise a new phone tree and to put Goldie Fisch and Sam N. on different branches.

"It's a sad commentary when people can't put aside their personal issues for the safety of their community," said Case. "Sheesh."

The new phone tree will be distributed within days.

Gender Lines Clear-Cut in Local *Boy*cott

In what locals are calling a genuine *boy*cott, gender lines are clear-cut: boys on one side and girls on the other.

Not only are local women and girls refusing to eat at Caffè Angelo, they're also refusing to patronize all male-owned businesses in Geyser Creek.

In response, Geyser Creek's men and boys are shunning female-owned establishments.

"Strangest thing I've ever seen," said barber Fisher Cutbait. "Men who haven't been in for a haircut in years are coming by the shop. Say they just want to support the guys in town."

"Fisher can have the men in this town," said Pearl O. Ster, owner of The Fountainhead Salon. "I'm *boy*cotting boy cuts."

Meanwhile, Juan A. Lone, president of First National Bank of Geyser Creek, rejected a loan request by Geyser Creek Postmaster Carrie N. Urmayle, who then directed her mail carriers to stop home delivery to male households.

"The dumb males in this town can pick up their own dumb mail," said Urmayle.

Business mail will not be interrupted.

Letter to the Editor

Dear Editor:

On behalf of the women and girls in this town, I'm writing to respond to Gil's recent letter in which he suggested renaming our town Guys "R" Creek.

Given your struggles with spelling, Gil, I can appreciate why this change appeals to you. So, for your convenience and that of your fellow spelling-challenged brothers, we will support the spelling change with a slight modification.

Henceforth, our town shall be spelled as follows: Guys, (It's) Her Creek.

Sincerely,

Shelly
Sixth-Grade Student
Guys, (It's) Her Creek Middle School

Now serving:

REAL MANicotti

LEAF THE TREES ALONE!
Please help me save the trees on our school campus.
Minnie O.

Ax not!
It's what you can do for your country.

Geyser Creek Cafe

Now delivering — to women and girls only.

GO Fisch!

Our-Philosophy-About-Men Salad: lettuce alone

Angel Fisch, Owner

ANNOUNCEMENT: I don't like the girls-versus-boys mentality in this classroom. I expect cooperation and civility from everyone toward everyone. <u>Mi capite?</u>

TODAY'S ASSIGNMENT: Let's research the history of May Day. How is it celebrated in various parts of the world?

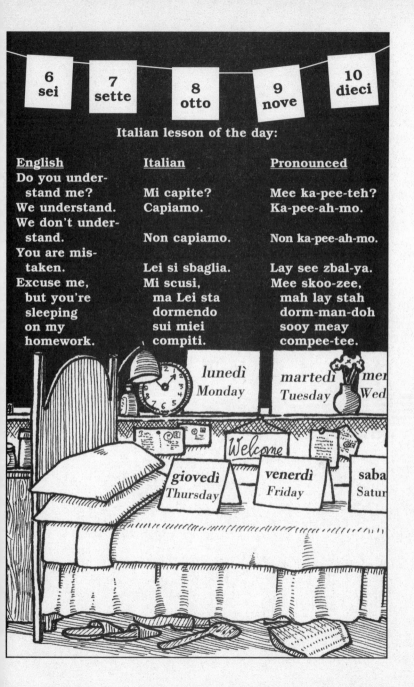

6 sei **7 sette** **8 otto** **9 nove** **10 dieci**

Italian lesson of the day:

English	Italian	Pronounced
Do you understand me?	Mi capite?	Mee ka-pee-teh?
We understand.	Capiamo.	Ka-pee-ah-mo.
We don't understand.	Non capiamo.	Non ka-pee-ah-mo.
You are mistaken.	Lei si sbaglia.	Lay see zbal-ya.
Excuse me, but you're sleeping on my homework.	Mi scusi, ma Lei sta dormendo sui miei compiti.	Mee skoo-zee, mah lay stah dorm-man-doh sooy meay compee-tee.

lunedì Monday

martedì Tuesday

mer Wed

giovedì Thursday

venerdì Friday

saba Satur

Welcome

4/18

Mr. N.,

Non capisco today's announcement.
You and Goldie don't cooperate.
You don't even talk to each other
anymore.

Tad Poll

SAM N.

April 18

Tad:

Lei si sbaglia. Despite my personal feelings for her, I can work with Goldie. It's called being a professional and being a gentleman. I expect the same of you.

Please work with Lily on the May Day assignment.

Grazie.

Mr. N.

MAY DAY
By Lily and Tad

A Maypole is a skyward symbol of life.

In ancient Rome, May Day was celebrated by marching to the grotto of Egena, where Romans celebrated the revival of vegetation.

Egyptians celebrated the goddess of spring on May Day.

May Day is traditionally a day for outdoor festivals, often tied to agricultural rituals. In medieval Europe, villagers cut down a tree and sawed off the branches. What remained served as the village Maypole. Villagers decorated it with ribbons and flowers, symbolizing love, beauty and fertility.

In Germany boys plant May trees in front of their sweethearts' windows. In the Czech Republic boys decorate their girlfriends' windows with a Maypole. Obviously, the boys there are more thoughtful than the boys here.

Yeah, right.

Anglo-Saxons called May Day *Beltane* ("bright fire") and considered it the first day of summer. *Beltane* was a celebration of love and courtship. (<u>GROSS</u>.) Each village elected a young couple to act as the king and queen of May. People gathered flowers, danced around the Maypole, and spent nights in the forest, looking up at the stars.

In Switzerland a boy places a May pine tree under his sweetie's window. Once again, it's clear that boys *everywhere else* are nicer than the boys in Geyser Creek.

Or is it clear that the GIRLS everywhere ELSE are nice, which inspires the BOYS to do nice things for them in return?

Mayday is also the international radio-telephone signal word for distress.
Example: "Mayday, Mayday! I'm sitting next to TAD."

MR. N., I CANNOT WORK WITH LILY!

GEYSER CREEK MIDDLE SCHOOL
Geyser Creek, Missouri
Our NEW school motto: *Go with the Flo!*

Mr. Walter Russ
Principal

OVERNIGHT MAIL

April 18

Ms. Florence Waters
President
Flowing Waters Fountains, Etc.
Watertown, California

Dear Ms. Waters,

I have found the solution to our problem in the unlikeliest of places: on Mr. N.'s bulletin board.

Consider this: In medieval Europe villagers cut down a tree and sawed off the branches. What remained became the Maypole under which villagers celebrated love.

In other words, the weeping willow tree will serve as our Maypole. I'm considering making Maypoles of many of the walnut trees as well.

Please let me know if this change in plans will affect your fee. As I've mentioned, the evaluators are especially sensitive to graft.

With all due respect,

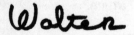

Walter Russ

P.S. I'm still very interested in the hall tree. So let's just settle down and concentrate on that, shall we?

68

Watertown, California

April 19

Wally Russ
The Principal Who Holds the Record for Being a Broken Record
Geyser Creek Middle School
Geyser Creek, Missouri

Settle down?

Wally, what if I don't want to settle down? *Ever.*

I agree. Outdoor weddings with Maypoles are lovely—if a person wants to get married in May under a pole.

But this person *doesn't.* Not for all the money in the *world.*

Wally, can I be honest with you? You're starting to worry me a little. And you're becoming a bit of a nag on this hall tree.

And why, pray tell, are the evaluators so sensitive to graft? You can do amazing things with graft. Have you never seen my All-in-One-Fruit-and-Nut Tree?

24	*Florence Waters Catalog of Fruit and Nut Trees*

The Florence Waters All-in-One-Fruit-and-Nut Tree

Florence Waters commits graft at her California nursery.

The apple-peach-pear-cherry-fig-banana-almond-cashew-pineapple tree!

That reminds me, Wally. I know you mentioned pruning your trees, but I'd like to apple and fig them, too. And I don't know how I can do that without some serious grafting.

Do you have any yew trees on your campus? I'd like to date a yew. But how many ways can I say this? I don't think I should date *you*, Wally.

I'm glad we've cleared this up!

Your *friend,*

Florence

Geyser Creek Middle School
Geyser Creek, Missouri

April 19

Florence Waters
President and CEO
Flowing Waters Fountains, Etc.
Watertown, California

Dear Florence,

Good news! I researched my family tree and
learned that I have roots in California. Maybe
my ancestors knew your ancestors.

The bad news is that none of the girls in our
class are talking to Tad or me. It's a drag
because I really like Shelly.

Ciao for now,

Gil

FLOWING WATERS FOUNTAINS, ETC.

Watertown, California

OVERNIGHT EXPRESS

April 20

Gil
c/o Mr. N.'s Sixth-Grade Class
Geyser Creek Middle School
Geyser Creek, Missouri

Dear Gil,

What fun to think our relatives might've known each other! If they did, I'm sure they were great friends.

So, Gil, I've been working on your ingenious idea for a picnic tree. I think I've almost got it. Just a few more branches to go!

Speaking of branches, may I suggest that you offer Shelly an olive branch? Giving someone an olive branch means making a gesture of peace. Try it! If you care for people, you have to show them.

That reminds me: Do you have an Italian suit? Every man needs at least one. The two I've enclosed should fit you and Tad.

Can't wait to see you in May! Till then,

Let the love ...

72

April 21

Dear Shelly,

I wish we could talk. We've been friends since kindergarten.

Would you like to have lunch with me? I'll bring us something from home if you don't want to eat at Caffè Angelo.

Is pb&j okay?

Gil

P.S. Florence sent Italian suits to Tad and me. We look sorta cool in them—if that's okay to say.

April 21

Dear Gil,

Thanks for the note. We've been friends forever and I hated being mad at you.

The problem is that if the other girls find out I'm not mad at you anymore, they'll be furious at me. We can be friends again. Just don't tell anyone, _va bene_?

Meet me under the weeping willow tree after school today. I can't stay long because I have to be at Minnie O.'s birthday party by four o'clock. But at least we can talk.

And of course I like pb&j! Almost as much as I like you—if that's okay to say.

Shelly

P.S. Can't wait to see your Italian dressing!

April 21

S:

Ha! And *va bene* about meeting under the weeping willow tree after school.

See you there.

G

P.S. I can't stay long, either. Tad and I are practicing a new song to play at the *caffè*.

✭THE GUYS, (IT'S) HER CREEK GAZETTE✭

Our NEW motto: "It's a girl thing!"

Friday, April 22	Early Edition	50 cents

Break-ins at *Caffè* and Cafe
Priceless recipes stolen!

Chef Angelo's secret trunk was damaged during the break-in.

Though burglars stole her recipe, Angel vows to wow Angelo in the cook-off.

Overnight break-ins at Geyser Creek Cafe and Caffè Angelo have left two local chefs without their most prized recipes.

At Geyser Creek Cafe, thieves took nothing but Angel Fisch's great-great-great-aunt Starr's recipe for macaroni and cheese. Similarly, Chef Angelo's great-great-grandfather's recipe for *penne ai quattro formaggi* was stolen from the trunk he keeps locked in the sixth-grade classroom.

The only witnesses were two sixth-grade boys who were walking around the Geyser Creek town square and playing Italian music at approximately 8:00 p.m.

"We've been working as strolling musicians at Caffè Angelo," said Tad Poll. "So we were practicing walking and playing at the same time. It's harder than it sounds."

Poll said that he and fellow sixth grader Gil heard noises coming from Geyser Creek Cafe, followed minutes later by the sound of giggling under the giant weeping willow tree behind Geyser Creek Middle School. The boys followed the sound of the voices, but the gigglers disappeared.

Sheriff Mack Rell said it is unknown if the break-ins at the *caffè* and the cafe are related. Nor will authorities say if the graffiti carved into the giant weeping willow tree is connected to the burglaries. (See story on page 2.)

What is clear is that the break-ins could not have come at a worse time for the two chefs, who are scheduled to prepare these recipes for a cook-off on May 1.

"This is my family tragedy," Chef Angelo said. "But I say we go straight ahead to the conflict. I can cook by the heart."

For once Fisch agreed with Angelo.

"On with the dadgum cook-off!" Fisch flouted as she popped a wheelie on her scooter.

Late Fees* Waived for Women and Girls!

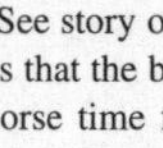

CeCe Salt, Librarian
Geyser Creek Public Library

*Fines doubled for men and boys.

Graffitree at Middle School

Another reason to eliminate the trees, says Russ

Weeping willow now boasts amorous message.

"S LOVES G," according to whoever carved the message into the weeping willow tree behind Geyser Creek Middle School.

But Principal Walter Russ doesn't love graffiti.

"Graffiti in any form will not be tolerated on school property," Russ told the *Gazette*. "Fortunately, the weeping willow tree will be cut down and decorated as part of our May Day celebration. Therefore, I do not intend to conduct an investigation or a determined hunt for the prankster or pranksters."

Russ says the graffiti on the giant weeping willow tree provides yet another reason to level it, and the entire walnut grove, on May 1.

"Clear-cutting the trees will be part of a wonderful May Day celebration," said Russ.

Meanwhile, Geyser Creek Middle School sixth grader Minnie O. is leafleting local homes and businesses with a "*Her*story of Our Trees" report.

"If people knew the real story about the trees on our school campus, they would leave the trees alone," said Minnie O.

Though she did not directly criticize Principal Russ's plans to clear-cut the trees on the school campus, Minnie O. said, "Sometimes I wonder if Mr. Russ can see the forest for the trees."

Letter to the Editor

Dear Editor:

I am writing to suggest a just and lasting solution to the local gender war.

I propose we establish two zones: one for men and boys, called Guys "R" Creek; the other for women and girls, called Guys, (It's) Her Creek.

Both zones would be equal in all ways but would be separated by a wall or fence.

To this end, I am waiving my fee for all male clients seeking divorces from local women.

Just trying to help.

Barry Cuda
Attorney-at-Law
Guys "R" Creek

Phone Tree Still Has Knots

Last night's graffiti and break-ins at the *caffè* and cafe would have been the perfect test of Geyser Creek's new phone tree, says Geyser Creek Emergency Director Justin Case.

"Sadly, we're still experiencing resistance to the phone tree," Case explained. "The biggest knot is that people aren't reporting suspicious activities like they should."

Gil, a witness to the break-ins, defended his silence. "Tad and I didn't think there was anything suspicious about someone being in the cafe at night or people meeting under the weeping willow tree," Gil said. "That tree is a popular meeting place for people who, um, you know, sorta like each other or whatever."

Leave your legal problems to me.

BARRY CUDA

Attorney-at-Law
Sharks, Sharks, and Sharks
1-800-GO4BLOOD

Caffè Angelo

Now serving:

Fish Cut in Little Tiny Pieces, Then Cooked in Coarse Salt!

"Take that!"

Attention ALL residents of Geyser Creek:

Please use the new phone tree to report emergencies, disasters, and/or any suspicious activities that demand immediate action.

Thank you.

Justin Case
Geyser Creek Emergency Director

LEAF THE TREES ALONE!

Have you received your free copy of *"Her*story of Our Trees"?

If not, please contact Minnie O.

Geyser Creek Cafe

Today's special:

Men-Are-Pigs in a Blanket!

Angel Fisch, Owner

April 22

Gil!

I cannot _believe_ you stole Angel's recipe for macaroni and cheese _and_ carved our initials into the weeping willow tree!

I'm never speaking to you again.

Shelly

April 22

Shelly,

Oh, right. Blame ME for what YOU and the girls
did.

Stealing Angelo's recipe was bad enough. But
telling everyone you (S) love me (G)—on a *tree*?
And *you're* the one who said I wasn't supposed to
tell anyone.

I thought you'd at least be grateful that I didn't
tell the police the giggles I heard under the tree
were YOURS.

Gil

April 22

Gil:

My giggles? I wasn't even near school last night. After we met under the weeping willow tree, I went to Minnie O.'s birthday party. I was there until nine o'clock, making leaflets for the Leaf the Trees Alone campaign.

So now you're a liar _and_ you can't keep a secret. You make me want to visit a vomitorium. (Now there's a _real_ Italian invention for you.)

Why don't you be like a tree and _leave_ me alone?

    Shelly

P.S. For your information, I've never liked Italian dressing—on salad _or_ men.

April 22

Shelly,

Fine.

Arrivederci. (Forever)

Gil

OVERNIGHT MAIL

April 22

Ms. Florence Waters
President
Flowing Waters Fountains, Etc.
Watertown, California

Dear Ms. Waters,

Just a quick note to confirm that we're still on for May 1.

I'll confess I don't know anything about rings, but I'm told we should examine them—for posterity, if nothing else. I believe the rule of thumb is to measure the girth approximately three feet from the ground. Each circumference inch equals approximately one year.

In any case, I look forward to getting this matter resolved. I don't need to tell you how impressive—or dangerous—the limbs are. Needless to say, I'm concerned about possible injuries to life and the potential roof damage.

After the celebration, perhaps we can toast with a cup of coffee.

Sincerely,

Walter

Walter Russ

P.S. To answer your question: We have no yew trees on our campus.

'FLOWING WATERS FOUNTAINS, ETC.'

Watertown, California

April 23

Wally Russ
The Principal Who Is Just My Pal
Geyser Creek Middle School
Geyser Creek, Missouri

Dear Friend,

I'll admit my legs and arms are impressive. But *dangerous*?
Wally!

Look, I have nice limbs because I exercise every single day.
You'd have impressive limbs, too, if you'd move a little. Here
are some dance exercises from my new book, *Branch Out! New
Moves for Old Limbs*:

Branch Out! New Moves for Old Limbs

The Oak-y Pokey

The Boxwood Boxstep

The Mango Tango

The Don't-Cry-for-Me
Weeping Willow Waltz

The Kumquat Foxtrot

The I-Wanna-Hustle-
With-Yew!

Wally, you're adorable. But I don't want to look at rings with you, okay? Jewelry gets in my way.

And for future reference you should know that rings are not measured by the *inch* but by the *carat*. Also, please note that many women would take offense to the term *girth*.

Your F R I E N D,

P.S. If you want a maple, walnut, mahogany, pine, and spruce hall tree, *of course* you should be concerned about roof damage. Don't worry. I'm planning to take the roof off the school, anyway. It'll be easier that way.

P.P.S. Do you like bark? The chocolate kind, I mean. Seems a natural tree trimming, yes? Try the enclosed samples. Save a piece or two for our friend Leify.

white chocolate bark

dark chocolate bark

GEYSER CREEK MIDDLE SCHOOL
Geyser Creek, Missouri
Our NEW school motto: *Go with the Flo!*

Mr. Walter Russ
Principal

OVERNIGHT MAIL

April 25

Ms. Florence Waters
President
Flowing Waters Fountains, Etc.
Watertown, California

Ms. Waters,

Ha-ha. About taking the roof off, that is.

All I meant by the potential roof damage, Ms. Waters, is that you can be a little more aggressive, if you want.

Very truly yours,

Walter

Walter Russ

FLOWING WATERS FOUNTAINS, ETC.

Watertown, California

OVERNIGHT EXPRESS

April 26

Wally Russ
The Principal Who Could Use a Few Principles
Geyser Creek Middle School
Geyser Creek, Missouri

Wally!

Well, of course I could be a little more aggressive! And if I wanted to marry you, I *would* be more aggressive.

Oh, for pity's sake. You've worn me down. We can tie the knot after we trim the trees on May 1. But I will *not* celebrate the event with toast and a cup of coffee. Wally, please. If we're going to do this, let's do it *right*.

I'll plan the whole thing. Just show up in a tux, okay? And shine your shoes.

Are you happy now, Wally?

For better or for worse,

Florence

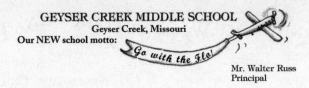

OVERNIGHT MAIL

April 27

Ms. Florence Waters
President
Flowing Waters Fountains, Etc.
Watertown, California

Dear Ms. Waters,

What a load off my mind. Thank you!

I like your idea of tying the knot after trimming the trees. I'm assuming you mean we'll use ribbons to decorate the tree stumps. Blue ribbons might be nice. I'll leave the details to you.

See you on May 1. I have some axes to grind in the meantime.

Yours sincerely,

Walter

Walter Russ

TELL-A-GRAM

The Old-Timey Telegram Company

Sent to: A. Trap
Editor, The Geyser Creek Gazette
Geyser Creek, Missouri

Sent from: F. Waters
Watertown, California

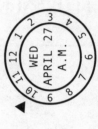

WED
APRIL 27
A.M.

WEDDING OF THE CENTURY TO TAKE PLACE ON MAY FIRST - STOP -
WALLY MY CUTIE-PATOOTIE CAN FILL YOU IN ON DETAILS - STOP -
ALL OF GEYSER CREEK INVITED - STOP - NO PRESENTS - STOP - JUST
EVERYONE'S PRESENCE PLEASE - STOP - CEREMONY TO BE HELD ON
MIDDLE SCHOOL GROUNDS AT ONE MINUTE AFTER MIDNIGHT - STOP -
FLORENCE WATERS

FORM 1807

⋆THE GUYS, (IT'S) HER CREEK GAZETTE⋆

Our NEW motto: "It's the *strangest* thing!"

Wednesday, April 27	Late Edition	50 cents

FLORENCE WATERS TO MARRY WALTER

Bride-to-be Florence Waters

The ungroomed groom Walter Russ

In a surprising (okay, downright *shocking*) development, world-famous fountain designer, artist, and author Florence Waters has announced plans to marry Geyser Creek Middle School Principal Walter Russ on May Day.

Waters notified the *Gazette* of the happy (some might say *jaw-dropping*) news by telegram earlier today.

Everyone in Geyser Creek is invited to the wedding, which will take place at one minute after midnight on Sunday, May 1, on the grounds of Geyser Creek Middle School.

Honeymoon plans have not been announced. The newlyweds will have to wait until the completion of Walter Russ's evaluation by Leif Blite from the Society of Principals and Administrators. The evaluation is also scheduled for May 1.

Will Wedding Put a Stop to Local *Boy*cott?

Could Florence Waters's marriage to Walter Russ put an end to Geyser Creek's *boy*cott?

Sure, say some. Maybe, say others. No way, says beauty salon owner Pearl O. Ster.

"When I heard Florence was going to marry Wally, you could've knocked me over with a feather boa," Ster said. "But just because she's tying the knot doesn't mean we're giving up the *boy*cott."

According to Ster, Geyser Creek's women and girls should sit on the left side of the aisle, traditionally reserved for friends and family of the bride. Men and boys should sit on the right side.

"Guess that proves men are right," said barber Fisher Cutbait.

Caffè Angelo

Now serving:

Lasagna-na-na-na!

Phone Tree Not for Gossip or "Cold Feet," Says Justin Case

After receiving several calls to the phone tree to report the upcoming wedding of Florence Waters and Walter Russ, Geyser Creek Emergency Director Justin Case issued the following reminder:

"Please use the phone tree to report emergencies and suspicious activities only," Case said. "It's not intended for local gossip."

A review of calls made to the phone tree indicates that one of today's repeat callers was Walter Russ.

"Wally said it was a matter of life or death," said Case. "I told him that till-death-do-us-part stuff is scary, but it's not an *emergency* in the official sense of the word. Besides, most guys get cold feet before their weddings."

Break-ins at *Caffè* and Cafe Still Unsolved

Something Fischy about the school burglary, says sheriff.

Last Thursday's break-ins at Geyser Creek Cafe and Caffè Angelo remain a mystery, said Geyser Creek Sheriff Mack Rell.

"But we have identified a partial set of local fingerprints in Mr. N.'s room near Angelo's trunk," said Rell.

Though he refused to finger the fingerprinter, Rell said, "There's something Fischy going on here."

BE-*LEAVE* IN THE TREES!

Please help save the trees
at our school.

Minnie O.
Founder, Leaf the Trees Alone

Letter to the Editor

Dear Editor:

I am writing in response to Barry Cuda's proposal that we establish separate zones for men and women in this town.

As any credible lawyer would know, the concept of separate but equal has long been abandoned as patently unjust.

Therefore, I am preemptively banning any such dividing walls and/or fences in this town, and I'm revoking Barry Cuda's license to practice law.

Just trying to be fair.

Judge Anne Chovey
Circuit Court
Guys, (It's) Her Creek, MO

Geyser Creek Cafe

**This week: *Chic Joannes*
(formerly known as Sloppy Joes)**

GO FISCH!

Angel Fisch, Owner

Please call the phone tree to report any emergency situation or suspicious activity.

Justin Case
Geyser Creek Emergency Director

GEYSER CREEK MIDDLE SCHOOL
Geyser Creek, Missouri
Our NEW school motto:

Mr. Walter Russ
Principal

FAX

DATE: April 27
TO: Annette Trap
FR: Walter Russ
RE: Erratum

Ms. Trap:

Please advise your readers immediately that I do NOT plan to marry Florence Waters.

Instead of *wedding*, I'm sure Ms. Waters meant to write that a *weeding* will take place on May 1.

As you know, Ms. Waters is coming to town to trim the unsightly trees on our school campus. One of these trees has not been trimmed for 100 years. Hence, it will be the *weeding* of the century.

After Ms. Waters and I eliminate the ancient weeping willow tree, we will hold a traditional May Day celebration. I borrowed that idea from Mr. N.'s class. We're adding something new, though: decorative blue ribbons tied to the knotty trunks and felled limbs.

Everyone is invited to attend this "tying of the knot," which I know will be a gala occasion.

Please advise your readers accordingly. Any confusion on this point could be embarrassing to all involved.

Thank you.

Walter Russ

Walter Russ

DATE _____
TO _____

DATE April 27 HOUR 2:40pm
TO Mr. Russ

WHILE YOU WERE OUT

Mr. Annette Trap still single
OF The Geyser Creek Gazette
PHONE 746-4301

☒ Telephoned ☐ Returned Call ☐ Left Package
☐ Please Call ☐ Was In ☐ Please See Me
☐ Will Call Again ☐ Won't Call ☐ Important

MESSAGE: Annette Trap said
in future editions of the
Gazette she'll refer to
your wedding, as a "tying
of the knot." She also
said she's glad you're
using something old, new,
borrowed, and blue in the
ceremony.
Signed Goldie T.

GEYSER CREEK MIDDLE SCHOOL
Geyser Creek, Missouri
Our NEW school motto: *Go with the Flo!*

Mr. Walter Russ
Principal

FAX

DATE: April 27
TO: Leif Blite
FR: Walter Russ
RE: My evaluation

Mr. Blite:

I'm writing to alert you to a certain development here that is ...
Well, it's *amusing*, really. That's what it is–amusing!

In fact, one could chuckle to oneself when one imagines the possible appearance of impropriety. Why, if one didn't know better,
one might think that one's relationship with one's contractor had
gone wildly off course, when in fact, one never had any intentions
regarding anything other than tidying up the trees on one's school
campus so that one could pass one's evaluation.

In conclusion, when do you plan to arrive in town, sir?

Walter Russ

Walter Russ

SOCIETY OF PRINCIPALS AND ADMINISTRATORS

Making the World Safe for Bureaucracy

10 Maple Leaf Plaza   Washington, D.C.

FACSIMILE

DATE: April 27
TO: Walter Russ
FR: Leif Blite
RE: Your evaluation

Mr. Russ:

Have you gone barking mad?

I arrive in Geyser Creek the day after tomorrow. I'll pick up
your correspondence file then. Your evaluation will begin first
thing on Sunday, May 1.

One hopes you have identified other job opportunities.

Leif Blite

Leif Blite
Branch Chief, Evaluators of Lower Midwest (ELM)

LEAF THE TREES ALONE

OUR MISSION: TO SAVE THE TREES AT GEYSER CREEK MIDDLE SCHOOL

MINNIE O., FOUNDER AND PRESIDENT

April 27

Florence Waters
The Bride-to-Be!
Flowing Waters Fountains, Etc.
Watertown, California

Dear Florence,

I really don't know what to say, except...WOW! And congratulations!!!!!

I think you should have your wedding under the weeping willow tree. If you did, then Wally wouldn't have the heart to cut it down. (Would he?)

It wouldn't be the first time someone got married under the weeping willow tree. Take a look at this! ⟶

Minnie O.

MINUTES FROM THE MEETING OF THE MAIDS OF MAY

Ten members attended the May meeting, which began with the composition and recitation of verses 85 and 86 of the Maids Pledge:

> We are the Maids of May—
> Who celebrate our ancestry
> By planting trees for others
> From here to Tripoli.
>
> Have you ever noticed how
> A Maid of May is like a tree?
> With every year she grows older,
> She gains more dignity.

After reading and approving the minutes from our last meeting, we discussed old business, including our field trip to the Kalahari Desert, where we planted 200 cacti. Later, we rented motorcycles and toured Morocco by bike, with picnics at every stop.

Merry Marrakech!

Our meeting concluded with refreshments, which we enjoyed while looking at photographs sent from the former Miss Wilhomena Furr, who recently married Will U. Merrame. The happy couple held their wedding ceremony under the giant weeping willow. Veteran Maids will recall that these are the children (now 28 years old!) who planted the walnut saplings for us along the banks of Spring Creek.

Will U. and Wilhomena Merrame

Respectfully submitted,

April Showers

April Showers
Secretary, Maids of May

GO-WITH-THE-FLO EXPRESS — SAME-DAY SERVICE

April 28

Ms. Minnie O.
c/o Sam N.'s Sixth-Grade Class
Geyser Creek Middle School
Geyser Creek, Missouri

Dear Minnie O.,

What a great idea to have the wedding under the weeping willow tree!

Can I count on you, Lily, Paddy, and Shelly to be the bridesmaids? We'll call you the Maids of May. Don't worry about the dresses. I know all your sizes and will bring gowns for everyone, including me. I can't remember the last time I wore a dress. Send ideas, please!

I'll admit I'm a little nervous about all this. I've thrown hundreds of parties, but I've never planned a wedding. If it's okay with you, I'll leave many of the details to you and your classmates. I'll handle the decorations.

Let's all meet under the tree at 10:30 Saturday night.

Eeps! That's just two days away! No time to waste. I'd better send this by GO-WITH-THE-FLO EXPRESS. You remember my pilot, A. V. Aytor, right? If you have more wedding information for me, send it back with her.

This will be FUN!

Love,

Florence

P.S. Do you think Mr. N., Gil, and Tad would be willing to serve as the groomsmen and ushers? Please deliver the enclosed notes to them and to the girls. Thanks, sweetie!

Shelly
Geyser Creek Middle School
Geyser Creek, MO
USA

Lily
~~Geyser~~ Creek Middle School
~~Geyser~~ Creek, MO

Paddy
Geyser Creek Middle School
Geyser Creek, MO
USA

Sam N.
Geyser Creek Middle School
Geyser Creek, MO
USA

Goldie Fisch
Geyser Creek Middle School
Geyser Creek, MO
USA

Tad
Geyser Creek Middle School
Geyser Creek, MO
USA

Gil
Geyser Creek Middle School
Geyser Creek, MO
USA

ANNOUNCEMENT: We have to plan a wedding!

TODAY'S ASSIGNMENTS:

- **Invitations:** *Paddy*
- **Food: Talk to Angel** (Lily) **and Angelo** (Tad)
- **Music:** Gil and Tad
- **Dresses: Send sketches to Florence** *Shelly*
- **Flowers:** *Paddy*
- **Venue:** *Minnie O.*
- **Contact Judge Anne Chovey to officiate: Gil**
- **Video:** Lily
- **Wedding license: Mr. N.**

Important: Please turn in all assignments to Goldie Fisch by 3:00 p.m. She'd like to see your ideas before we send them back to Florence.

Italian lesson of the day:

English	Italian	Pronounced
wedding	nozze	noh-tzeh
We're having a party.	Noi diamo un ricevimento.	Noy dya-mo oon ree-che-vee-men-to.
Would you like to come?	Vuol venire?	Vwol ve-neer-eh?
I'm sorry, Angelo, but we can't concentrate when you're singing opera.	Mi dispiace, Angelo, ma non riusciamo a concentrarci quando Lei canta l'opera.	Mee dees-peeah-chey, mah non ree-oo-see-ah-moh ah con-chayn-trahr-che goo-ahn-do lay cahn-tah lo-peh-ra.

April 28

Florence Waters
Fountain Designer and Fiancée
Flowing Waters Fountains, Etc.
Watertown, California

Florence,

I can't believe you're getting married—to Wally! I want to hear the whole story when you get here.

Of course I'd be honored to be a bridesmaid! I hope you're planning to live in Geyser Creek after the wedding. Maybe you can be principal when Wally gets fired. (Everyone says he probably will.)

Love,

Shelly

P.S. Here are my ideas for what we could all wear in the wedding.

2.

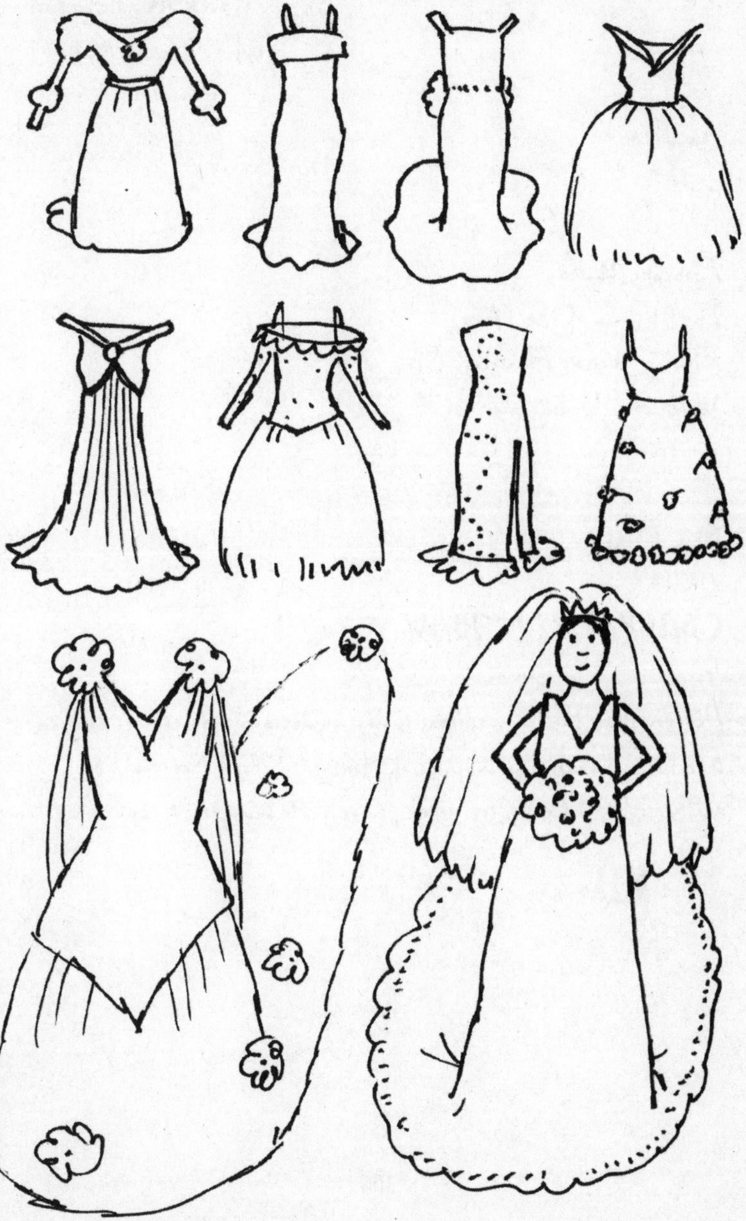

April 28

Florence Waters
The Woman of the Hour
Flowing Waters Fountains, Etc.
Watertown, California

Dear Florence,

CONGRATULATIONS!

Did you know that in medieval times, bridesmaids sometimes carried tree limbs rather than bouquets of flowers? I think that would be really cool. And easy, too, since you've got to trim the trees anyway.

Paddy

RAGAZZO

Geyser Creek Middle School
Geyser Creek, Missouri

April 28

Florence Waters
Bride2B
Flowing Waters Fountains, Etc.
Watertown, California

Dear Florence,

That's some news about you and Mr. Russ. Well, congratulations and all that stuff. Of course we'd be honored to be the ushers. We have the perfect suits, thanks to you!

We could also be your wedding musicians. How about if we play selections from Vivaldi's *The Four Seasons*? At the reception we could play Rossini's *The Barber of Seville*. Chef Angelo told us it's the best example of *opera buffa,* which he described as "the funny opera about how crazy the love it makes you." (Chef Angelo cracks us up!)

Did you know that Italians invented opera in about 1570? Back then it was sorta the Mediterranean equivalent to computer games. Everybody loved it.

See you on May 1, Mizz Bride!

Gil   Tad Poll

April 28

Florence Waters
Future Wife of Wally Russ
Flowing Waters Fountains, Etc.
Watertown, California

Dear Florence,

This is so fun and exciting!

Did you know Chef Angelo and Angel Fisch are holding their big cook-off on May 1? We can serve their food at the reception.

Here's what we're planning:

WEDDING RECEPTION MENU

From Caffè Angelo

Penne ai quattro formaggi

Radicchio con acciughe e capperi

Focaccia

Gelato

From Geyser Creek Cafe

Macaroni and cheese

Potato salad

Dinner rolls

Jell-O salad

The wedding cake is sorta tricky because both Angel and Angelo want to make it—*alone.* So we're having Angel bake the top two layers and Angelo the bottom two. We'll put it together like this:

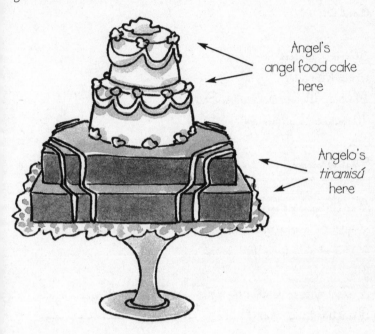

Angel's
angel food cake
here

Angelo's
tiramisú
here

Hope it looks okay to you!

Congratulations!

Lily

LEAF THE TREES ALONE

OUR MISSION: TO SAVE THE TREES AT GEYSER CREEK MIDDLE SCHOOL

MINNIE O., FOUNDER AND PRESIDENT

April 28

Florence Waters
Bride (Almost!)
Flowing Waters Fountains, Etc.
Watertown, California

Dear Florence,

I'm 100 percent excited about your wedding, but I'm also completely worried about the trees here at school. Principal Russ is dead set on cutting them down.

I might have to do what the Maids of May did 31 years ago. Read this to see what I mean. ──────────────→

What do you think?

  Minnie O.

MINUTES FROM THE MEETING OF THE MAIDS OF MAY

Seven members attended the May meeting, which began with the composition and recitation of verses 139 and 140 of the Maids Pledge:

> We are the Maids of May,
> Who care little what people say.
> Because worrying just gives you warts,
> And life is much too short!
>
> "O, ye Maids of May!
> Just what do you do all day?"
> Such a funny thing to say
> To us who live to play.

After reading and approving minutes from our last meeting, the Maids discussed old business, including our mahogany tree-planting trip to Machu Picchu, Peru, and the flying lessons we took while there. (Fun!)

Thereafter followed a discussion of the local campaign we sponsored earlier this year to prevent the walnut grove from being paved and the weeping willow tree cut down for the new middle school. Several maids shimmied up the graceful willow and lived in it for 14 days!

Maids save the day! Yay!

The Maids prevailed. No trees were destroyed in the construction of the new middle school, which is scheduled to open later this month.

Speaking of the middle school, we attach for our records a letter from former student Mrs. Wilhomena Furr Merrame.

Respectfully submitted,

Rosie Busch

Rosie Busch
Secretary, Maids of May

Dear Maids of May,

Thank you for leading the effort to save the lovely trees on the new middle school campus. As some of you might recall, I was one of the students who helped plant the walnut saplings way back when.

Isn't it strange and wonderful to see how tall the trees have grown since then? And to think I haven't aged a bit! (Well...)

Just want to let you know that we recently hosted a birthday party for our granddaughter Olivia under the weeping willow, where Will and I were married 27 years ago. Olivia is five years old and the daughter of my daughter, Willow. How time flies!

Fond regards,

Wilhomena Furr Merrame

112

TELL-A-GRAM

The Old-Timey Telegram Company

Sent to: Minnie O.
Sixth-Grade Student
Geyser Creek, Missouri

Sent from: F. Waters
Watertown, California

FRI
APRIL 29
A.M.

AMAZING - STOP - WOULD YOU BE WILLING TO GO OUT ON A LIMB TO

HELP AN OLD FRIEND - STOP - YOU KNOW WHAT I MEAN RIGHT - STOP -

FLO

✶THE GUYS, (IT'S) HER CREEK GAZETTE✶

Our NEW motto: "It's a wedding thing!"

Saturday, April 30   **Late Edition**   **50 cents**

Florence Waters and Walter Russ to Tie Knot Tomorrow
Trees to be trimmed as part of ceremony

Sixth graders make final wedding preparations.

The groom practices his line: "I do."

Plans are on track for Florence Waters and Walter Russ to tie the knot tomorrow, according to event planners from Sam N.'s sixth-grade class at Geyser Creek Middle School.

"Florence asked our class to handle all the details," said Shelly, one of Waters's four bridesmaids. School secretary Goldie Fisch will be the maid of honor.

"Florence sent me a note," Fisch confirmed. "She's even bringing me a dress to wear. She really is an amazing friend."

Sixth-grade teacher Sam N. received a similar note from Waters.

"She told me I was the obvious pick for best man," Mr. N. said with a chuckle. "I'm to wear my best suit and shine my shoes."

The ceremony will begin at 12:01 a.m. under the giant weeping willow tree behind Geyser Creek Middle School.

Meanwhile, Principal Russ said he remains committed to cutting down the weeping willow as part of the wedding, which he insists on calling "a simple tying of the knot by Ms. Waters and myself."

Asked if he planned to refer to Florence as "Ms. Waters" even after the ceremony, Mr. Russ said: "I do." (See related wedding story, p. 2.)

Evaluator Arrives in Geyser Creek
Principal Russ could get the ax

Leif Blite arrives in Geyser Creek.

Leif Blite, branch chief from the Society of Principals and Administrators, arrived in Geyser Creek yesterday. Blite is in town to evaluate the administration of Geyser Creek Middle School Principal Walter Russ.

Although the evaluation is routine, Blite admitted that the Society of Principals and Administrators has serious questions about Russ's administration.

"Our concerns are primarily regarding the fountain, regarding the sink, and now, based on recent correspondence from Principal Russ, regarding the trees on the middle school campus," said Blite, who visited the school on Friday.

Asked if he worries he could lose his job as a result of a poor evaluation, Principal Russ said: "I do."

Principal Russ Up a Tree Over Student Up a Tree

Student activist moves into tree in attempt to save it.

The timing couldn't be worse for Geyser Creek Middle School Principal Walter Russ.

Already juggling his all-important evaluation by the Society of Principals and Administrators and his tying of the knot with Florence Waters, Russ now has the added complication of a student who refuses to come down from the giant weeping willow tree on the middle school campus.

With only a backpack filled with food, water, and reading materials, Minnie O., founder of the Leaf the Trees Alone campaign and daughter of Dr. Sandy Beech, moved into the tree late last night.

Minnie O., who recently turned 12 years old, stated her goal: "To prevent Principal Walter Russ from cutting down the 100-year-old tree."

Asked if he worries that the student protestor will reflect badly on his administration, Russ said: "I do."

Letter to the Editor

Dear Editor:

I am writing to tell everyone that effective immediately, I'm moving onto the highest limb of the beautiful old weeping willow tree behind the middle school. I will not leave the tree until Principal Russ promises not to cut it down.

I'm sorry if this seems drastic. I'm just trying to help an old friend.

Minnie O.
Sixth-Grade Student
Geyser Creek Middle School

Old, New, Borrowed and Blue
Ceremony will include traditional, nontraditional elements
(Just don't call it a *wedding*)

Though details of the, um, *event* are sketchy, the *Gazette* has learned that Walter Russ will incorporate the traditional elements of something old, something new, something borrowed and something blue in tomorrow's ceremony.

Standing tall (for now) at 100 years old, the weeping willow tree under which the ceremony will take place is clearly something old. The tying of blue ribbons around the felled tree will provide something new and something blue. And using a traditional May Day celebration as the theme for the reception was an idea borrowed from Mr. N.'s sixth-grade class, Principal Russ said.

Still, Russ insisted the ceremony would be a *weeding*, not a *wedding*.

"Ms. Waters and I are simply tying the knot," Russ told the *Gazette* yesterday.

What*ever*, Wally!

The Fountainhead Salon

"You're not wearing *that* to the wedding, are you?"

Last-minute wedding hairdos and fashion advice
Women and Girls ONLY

Pearl O. Ster, Owner

Caffè Angelo

May Day Cook-Off

"Please, you will vote for me, yes?"

Geyser Creek Cafe

GO FISCH!

"Folks, don't miss the cook-off!"

Angel Fisch, Owner

Geyser Creek Barbershop

Wedding Dos and Don'ts

Fisher Cutbait, Barber

"No hairspray, guys. I promise."

FACSIMILE

DATE: April 30
TO: Walter Russ
FR: Leif Blite
RE: Your so-called "school"

Mr. Russ:

Yesterday afternoon I paid an unannounced visit to Geyser
Creek Middle School, where I observed monkeys roaming
the hallways; a cafeteria sink filled with live fish; an alleged
"drinking fountain," in which students were not only quench-
ing their thirst with assorted juices and milk shakes but were
also swimming, snorkeling, ice-skating, and feeding the
exotic birds that reportedly live in or near the fountain.
Unprovoked, a big swan snapped at me.

While tending this injury, I observed a pair of sixth-grade
boys parading down a hallway, singing opera arias while
their female counterparts delivered class assignments and
lunch to a child who apparently is living in a tree—not to be
confused with the Italian chef who's living in the sixth-grade
classroom.

I'll admit the children were polite. To wit: They invited me
to your wedding ceremony tomorrow.

Also while at the school, I retrieved your correspondence
file. Additional comment would be superfluous.

Leif Blite

Leif Blite
Branch Chief, Evaluators of Lower Midwest (ELM)

GEYSER CREEK MIDDLE SCHOOL
Geyser Creek, Missouri
Our NEW school motto: *Go with the Flo!*

Mr. Walter Russ
Principal

FAX

DATE: April 30
TO: Leif Blite c/o Geyser Creek Inn
FR: Walter Russ
RE: My so-called "future"

Mr. Blite:

I have resigned myself to getting fired. I ask only that you extend me the professional courtesy of not giving me the ax in public.

If I must leave my office, I'd like to do so quietly and with what little dignity I have left.

Thank you.

Walter Russ

Walter Russ

P.S. For your information, I have no plans to marry Florence Waters tomorrow.

P.P.S. None. Zero. Not a chance. Never. Not me. No siree!

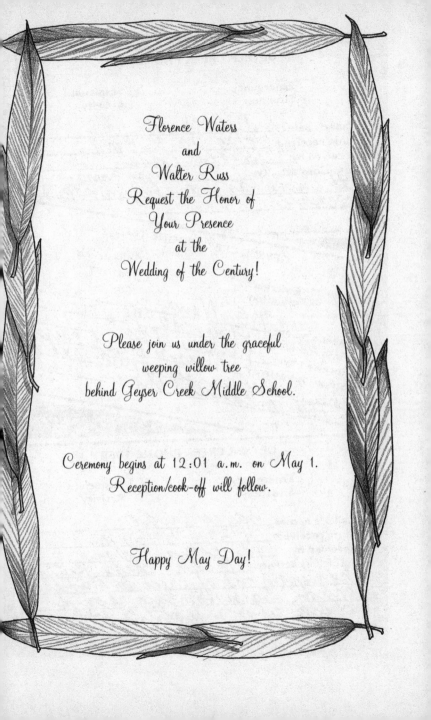

Florence Waters
and
Walter Russ
Request the Honor of
Your Presence
at the
Wedding of the Century!

Please join us under the graceful
weeping willow tree
behind Geyser Creek Middle School.

Ceremony begins at 12:01 a.m. on May 1.
Reception/cook-off will follow.

Happy May Day!

GEYSER CREEK PHONE TREE

☐ Emergency
Situation

☑ Suspicious
Activity

Caller's name: _CeCe Salt_
Time received: _4/30, 10:36 p.m._
Received by: _Justin Case_
Suspicious activity: _CeCe says something's up at the middle school._

GEYSER CREEK PHONE TREE

☑ Suspicious
Activity

☐ Emergency
Situation

Caller's name: _I.B. Newt_
Time received: _4/30, 10:45 p.m._
Received by: _Justin Case_
Suspicious activity: _Mazor Newt says he hears a helicopter over the middle school._

GEYSER CREEK PHONE TREE

☐ Emergency
Situation

☑ Suspicious
Activity

Caller's name: _Barry Cuda_
Time received: _4/30, 11:15 p.m._
Received by: _Justin Case_
Suspicious activity: _Cuda says kids hanging out of trees at middle school. Says someone should check school's liability policy._

GEYSER CREEK PHONE TREE

☑ **Emergency Situation** ☐ **Suspicious Activity**

Caller's name: _Pearl O. Ster_
Time received: _4/30, 11:22 p.m._
Received by: _Justin Case_
Suspicious activity: _Pearl's mad as a hornet. Says it sounds like wedding reception's already started and she's just putting in her hot rollers._

GEYSER CREEK PHONE TREE

☑ **Emergency Situation** ☐ **Suspicious Activity**

Caller's name: _Operator_
Time received: _4/30, 11:56 p.m._
Received by: _Justin Case_
Suspicious activity: _MAYDAY! MAYDAY! Calls to phone tree are stressing trunk lines nationwide. FCC Chairperson Ken I. Cawlueback_

Suspicious activity: _has issued a cease-and-desist order on Geyser Creek phone tree._

THE WEDDING VIDEO

Transcript

Judge Anne Chovey: Dearly beloved, before we begin I want to personally welcome Minnie O. down from the weeping willow tree. Are you okay, kiddo?

Minnie O.: Yes, Judge Chovey. I'm fine.

Judge Anne Chovey: Okay, then let's get down to business.

Leif Blite: Hear! Hear!

Judge Anne Chovey: We are gathered here in the first hour of the first day of May to witness the union of Florence Waters and Walter Russ in marriage.

Walter Russ: Now wait just a dadgum minute. I never—

Florence Waters: Wally, honey, I'll handle this.

Walter Russ: But—

Judge Anne Chovey: Hush, Wally. In the interest of time, I've been asked by the bride to skip the traditional opening and jump right to the heart of the matter. And so I ask you, Florence Waters: Will you have this man, Walter Russ, to be your wedded husband? Will you love, comfort, honor, and keep him, in sickness and in health, as long as you both shall live?

Florence Waters: Well, now. What an *interesting* question! But when I said skip ahead to the good stuff, I meant the bit about if anyone objects to all this, speak now.

Judge Anne Chovey: Oh, all right. If anyone here knows a reason why these two should not be married, speak now or forever hold your peace.

Sam N.: I know a reason.

(SOUND OF GASPS)

Judge Anne Chovey: You're objecting to this union, Sam? On what grounds?

122

Sam N.: On school grounds, of course. But also on the grounds that Florence and Mr. Russ aren't getting married today.

Walter Russ: What a relief! No offense, Ms. Waters.

Florence Waters: None taken, Wally dear.

Walter Russ: Since no one's getting married, I suggest we—

Sam N.: Wait. I'm getting married.

Goldie Fisch: Me, too.

Walter Russ: What the—?

Sam N.: You look so beautiful, Goldie.

Goldie Fisch: Thanks, sweetie. You're a knockout in that suit. Okay, Judge. Can we start over with the vows? We've written our own.

Judge Anne Chovey: Go ahead.

Goldie Fisch: Hold my hand, Sam. I'm nervous. Okay, here goes. I, Goldie, take you, Sam, to be my husband, knowing in my heart of hearts that you will continue to be my best friend and my one true love. I promise to love, honor, and respect you; to comfort and support you each and every day; to laugh, cry, and grow with you. I promise to always be open and honest with you, and to cherish you as long as we both shall live. I mean, if that's what you want—if *I'm* who you want.

Sam N.: *Who I want?* Goldie, I'm head over heels in love with you. You're the most beautiful woman I've ever seen. And when you're 110 years old, you'll be just as beautiful as you are right now. Why? Because your beauty is driven by kindness, warmth, and truth. I love you not just for who you are but for who I am when I'm with you. I love your sensible sweaters. I love how you make me laugh. I love how you make everyone feel so special without a word or a gesture, but just by being yourself. Everything you promise me, I promise you. I will be honest and faithful to you. I will respect, trust, help, and care for you. I want to share my life with you through the best and worst of what lies ahead. I'm going to love you for the rest of your life, no matter what. I want to grow a family tree with you. Goldie, I pine for you.

Goldie Fisch: Oh, Sam.

Sam N.: Goldie … This is where we kiss—right, Judge?

Judge Anne Chovey: Hold on a second. We're not done yet. If anyone here knows a reason why these two should not be married now, speak now or forever hold your peace and we'll get on with the reception.

Chef Angelo: This cannot yet be!

Sam N.: What?

Chef Angelo: I cannot hold my peas.

Goldie Fisch: Angelo, why?

Chef Angelo: Because I want to marry, too.

Judge Anne Chovey: You do? Who?

Chef Angelo: The love of my life—Angel Fisch.

Angel Fisch: Angelo!

Chef Angelo: It is a truth! I can no longer live this lie. I love you from the first moment I see you in your little Go Fisch costume.

Angel Fisch: You did?

Chef Angelo: Of course! And when you appear every day at lunchtime in my *caffé*? My heart, it flip the flop.

Angel Fisch: It does?

Chef Angelo: Of course! And I have another confession. The person who break into your cafe? It was me.

Angel Fisch: But why?

Chef Angelo: Your Jell-O salad. And your macaroni with the cheese recipe. I make it for the cook-off.

Angel Fisch: I made *your* recipe for *penne ai quattro formaggi*.

Chef Angelo: What?! Where do you find my recipe?

Angel Fisch: Um … Well … I sorta broke into your trunk. Sorry.

Chef Angelo: That was you? Ha! A woman after my heart—and my recipes. You are the woman of great passion!

124

Angel Fisch: I do what I can.

Chef Angelo: I must marry you, my Angel, my beauty, my love, my—

Tad: This is getting *al musho*.

Chef Angelo: *Mi scusi*. But this is the woman of my every dream. I want to spend the rest of my days with you, my Angel.

Angel Fisch: Do you really love my Jell-O salad?

Chef Angelo: I do.

Angel Fisch: And my mushy pasta?

Chef Angelo: I do!

Angel Fisch: I want to keep my own last name.

Chef Angelo: Of course you do!

Angel Fisch: Do you agree to always help with the dishes?

Chef Angelo: I do!

Angel Fisch: And do you promise to always share the kitchen with me?

Chef Angelo: I…I…*Aye-yi-yi*. But okay. For you? I do!

Angel Fisch: And will you—

Goldie Fisch: Angel! He loves you, dangit. Let's get on with it!

Angel Fisch: Okay, okay. Judge, stay right where you are. There's going to be another wedding. Goldie, you'll be my maid of honor, right?

Goldie Fisch: Of course, honey. Back to you, Judge.

Judge Anne Chovey: Before I begin, is there anyone else who plans to get married here?

Gil: Yeah. Me.

(SOUND OF GASPS)

Sam N.: Gil!

Gil: Well, I do. I want to marry Shelly. Someday.

Shelly: My mom says I can't fall in love until I'm 21. But Gil, I want you to know I really, really like you. And I'm sorry for being so mean lately.

Gil: It's okay. Do you think we can be friends again?

Shelly: I do. Do you?

Gil: I do.

Judge Anne Chovey: Let the record reflect the above does not constitute an exchange of marital vows.

Leif Blite: Nicely put, Judge Chovey.

Judge Anne Chovey: Thank you, Mr. Blite. Where—*ahem*—was I? Oh yeah. Anybody else plan to get married today?

Fisher Cutbait: Pearl?

Pearl O. Ster: Don't even think about it, Fisher.

Fisher Cutbait: Rats. Never mind.

Judge Anne Chovey: Okay, let's continue. Florence, is there anything else you want me to say? Florence? Where's Florence?

(SOUND OF BELL RINGING)

Minnie O.: The hall tree! Florence must be ringing the new hall tree!

Walter Russ: The what?

✹THE GEYSER CREEK GAZETTE✹

Our NEW motto: "It's a LOVE thing!"

Sunday, May 1	Late Edition	50 cents

A TREEmendous May Day!

Three-ring circus at four-ring (plus a bell!) ceremony

Goldie and Sam wed just minutes before Angel and Angelo.	Angel and Angelo use macaroni as temporary wedding rings.	Even Leif Blite and Wally Russ exchange vows!	Wedding guests look on as newlyweds dance the willow waltz.

Whoops and sorry. (See erratum below.)

But who knew the real bride and groom at this morning's wedding would be Goldie Fisch and Sam N. instead of Florence Waters and Walter Russ? Or that Chef Angelo would propose to Angel Fisch during the ceremony, resulting in a second wedding?

Though at times as head-spinning as a three-ring circus, today's predawn four-ring ceremony and the reception that followed explained several recent puzzles around town, such as why Geyser Creek Middle School sixth-grade teacher Sam N. and school secretary Goldie Fisch refused to be on joining branches of the phone tree.

"We had become more than friends," said Sam N., who admitted carving *S* (for Sam) loves *G* (for Goldie) into the bark of the giant weeping willow tree behind the middle school.

"We knew if one of us called the other, we'd talk for hours and forget to call the next person on the list," explained Goldie Fisch-N.

The ceremony also included admissions by both Chef Angelo and Angel Fisch that each

had stolen the other's heart, not to mention each other's recipe for the cook-off.

No matter. When the moonlight reception began at approximately 12:30 a.m., the *boy*cott ended and everyone—boys, girls, men, women, even Leif Blite from the Society of Principals and Administrators—ate, danced and enjoyed the May Day celebration.

Before the wedding, sixth-grade student and Leaf the Trees Alone founder Minnie O. told Blite about his ancestor's involvement with the Maids of May.

"When Mr. Blite learned that it was his great-great-aunt Elm's idea to have students plant many of the trees on our school campus, he urged Wally not to touch them," explained Minnie O. "From there it was easy to negotiate a deal with Mr. Blite not to ax Wally if Wally didn't ax the trees."

After brokering the agreement between Russ and Blite, Minnie O. came down from her temporary home in the weeping willow tree to enjoy the weddings and the reception that followed.

(Continued on page 2, column 2)

Erratum: We regret the error in yesterday's edition of the *Gazette* that stated Florence Waters and Walter Russ would marry today. They did not marry, nor do they have plans to marry in the immediate future.

"But never say never," Waters said at the wedding reception.

Trick or *Tree-Eats*?
Trimmed trees offer tasty reception treats

When the wedding was through, guests enjoyed fondue.

Well, the trees got trimmed, all right.

But rather than chainsaw them down as Walter Russ requested, Florence Waters and her assistants from the sixth-grade class decorated the giant weeping willow tree and the entire walnut grove with a mouthwatering array of wedding treats, including fresh fruit, chocolates, nuts, cookies and marshmallows.

Small fondue burners were placed on reception tables so that guests could heat the chocolates, caramels and marshmallows to use as dipping sauces for the fruit, nuts and assorted breads and muffins. The baked goods arrived at eight o'clock in the morning for the hundreds of wedding guests who had stayed through the night and were ready for a light breakfast.

Waters said the idea for the tree trimmings came from a sixth-grade student.

"Gil sent me the brilliant idea for a picnic tree," explained Waters. "But we couldn't have properly trimmed the trees without Minnie O., who was brave enough to decorate the highest branches with caramels."

Though guests were dazzled by all of the *tree-eats*, Waters was disappointed with one of the trimmings.

"Wally wanted the trees pruned," Waters said. "But who wants a prune when you can have an apple dipped in warm caramel sauce?"

"I do," said Russ, still dizzy from the, um, *event*.

Blite Spares the Ax with Wally
(But cuts the rug with Judge Chovey!)

Leif Blite teaches Judge Anne Chovey "the ax."

Leif Blite said Geyser Creek Middle School Principal Walter Russ will receive a glowing recommendation "for his role in marrying academic administration with artistic expression, and for involving the irresistibly efficient Judge Anne Chovey in school activities."

After cutting the rug at the reception, Blite and Chovey enjoyed a power-breakfast meeting. Blite told the *Gazette* he planned to return to Geyser Creek to see Chovey and to research his family tree.

"I have roots here," said Blite, adding that he was suddenly fascinated by his local ties to Geyser Creek, both past and future.

MAY DAY *(Continued from page 1, column 2)*

As the newlywed couples enjoyed their first dance together, many of the wedding guests reported seeing the giant weeping willow tree gently sway in time to the music provided by two strolling musicians from the sixth-grade class at Geyser Creek Middle School.

Florence Waters, who was Goldie Fisch's maid of honor, toasted the couples by reminding them that by marrying they were intertwining the limbs of their family trees.

"That's why this is such a *tree*mendous occasion," Waters said. "Because trees can mend us. So can love."

Living Hall Tree to Replace Dead Phone Tree
Hall tree is Florence's "unwedding" gift for Wally

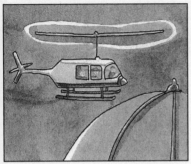

1. Florence Waters arrives (by helicopter).

2. Removes roof.

3. Lowers tree into hall.

Geyser Creek's phone tree was cut down by Ken I. Cawluback, chairperson of the Federal Communications Commission, who blamed the high volume of calls in Geyser Creek late last night for causing major trunk damage to the nation's phone lines.

Justin Case, Geyser Creek's emergency director, lost track of the number of incoming calls to the phone tree.

"It started shortly after 10:30 p.m.," said Case, explaining the commotion that accompanied Florence Waters's arrival at Gesyer Creek Middle School with a 75-foot African baobab tree.

"It's my 'unwedding' gift for Wally," said Waters when she unveiled the living hall tree after the wedding ceremony.

Waters, who removed the school roof, used a helicopter and a crane to transplant the hall tree outside Principal Walter Russ's office.

"That explains all the noise," said Case.

According to Waters, the hall tree has plenty of branches on which to hang coats and sweaters. "I've also hung a bell at the very top and attached a cable at the bottom," she said, explaining how the hall-tree bell can be used as both a school bell and a community alarm system.

Waters suggested Chef Angelo and Angel Fisch open a restaurant under the hall tree. She also showed how a portion of the massive tree had been excavated, with a small apartment built inside the tree. "Maybe Angelo and Angel could live here," she suggested.

The newlyweds jumped at the chance to live in the tree and announced plans to merge their eateries under it.

"It's because of Florence that I meet the woman of my dreams," said Chef Angelo.

Angel Fisch agreed. "When we get back from our honeymoon, Angelo and I are going to open Caffè Florence," she said. "I can't wait to learn how to make all those Italian classics!"

"But my sweet Angel," said Angelo, "now I like to make only the American food."

A heated discussion followed, interrupted only by a toast by Florence Waters: "May Angel and Angelo live, love, cook and argue happily ever after!"

The Fountainhead Salon

**Celebrate Your Roots at
The Fountainhead!**

**Now accepting appointments for
boys and men**

"I'm turning over a new leaf, friends."

Pearl O. Ster, Owner

There's something for everyone at the
GEYSER CREEK HIS, HERS, AND THEIRS-TORICAL SOCIETY

We Dig Your Roots!

Jeannie Ologee, Director

Geyser Creek Public Library

**Okay, ladies, let's get those
overdue books in.**

Guys, no more double fines.

Letter to the Editor

Dear Editor:

    Sure, it's nice to be a guy. But where would we be without the ladies?

    So, by special proclamation, I hereby suggest we honor the women and girls of this town by renaming it, as they suggested, Guys, (It's) Her Creek.

Respectfully submitted,

I. B. Newt
Mayor
Guys, (It's) Her Creek, MO

*Editor's note: Thanks, I.B., but the ladies and I
have decided we'd like to go back to calling it
Geyser Creek. That okay with everybody?*
    Annette Trap, Editor,
    The Geyser Creek Gazette

*Sign up now
for
summer school
at*
GEYSER CREEK MIDDLE SCHOOL

*We put the <u>cool</u>
in summer <u>school!</u>*

BARRY CUDA

**Thanks to Judge Anne
Chovey for reinstating
my law license!**

SAM N. and GOLDIE FISCH-N.

May 2

Florence Waters
Amica (Friend)
Flowing Waters Fountains, Etc.
Watertown, California

Dear Florence,

You did it again—left town before we could thank you.

Then again, how could we ever thank you enough? You planted the seed for our budding relationship and then rooted for us as our love grew.

Hope you understand why we had so little time to write last month. Falling in love and keeping it a secret kept us busy. Thank goodness for the weeping willow tree. That's where we had our April Fool's Day lunch date and our subsequent moonlight picnics. It's the most romantic spot in town!

With thanks and love,

Sam + Goldie

P.S. You weren't serious about the wedding gift, were you?

May 4

Sam N. and Goldie Fisch-N.
c/o Geyser Creek Middle School
Geyser Creek, Missouri

Dear Sam and Goldie,

Understand? I like to think I get a little credit for your romance.

Why do you suppose I brought Angelo to Geyser Creek? I knew he'd be a delicious distraction from you two—though I had no idea he and Angel would hit it off so famously. I knew that all I had to do was keep Wally nuts, and the two of you would be home free.

Of course I was serious about the wedding gift. I invited Angel and Angelo, too—and my favorite sixth-grade class. Plane tickets are on your desk, Goldie. I booked the flights for the first day of summer vacation. My villa in Florence is modest, but there's plenty of room (and privacy!) for everyone.

Love, love, love!

Flo

P.S. Sorry I had to dash before the reception was over. I was chaperoning Leify on his first date with Judge Chovey. *Someone* had to steer the conversation away from meetings, memos, and administrative mumbo-jumbo!

June 2

Florence Waters
Hostess with the Mostest
c/o Flowing Waters Fountains, Etc.
    Italian Branch Office
Florence, Italy

Hi, Florence!

Thought you'd enjoy seeing photos from our trip.

Living *la dolce vita*—or "the sweet life"—at your villa in Florence!

Here we are planting olive trees at Villa Florence.

We loved the gelato at Angelo's family's *ristorante*.

Arrivederci, Roma!
Thanks for telling us to throw a coin in the Trevi fountain!

Florence, we wish you could've come back to Geyser Creek with us. Do you know what we decided? You're like a tree because we can always lean on you, even though you always *leave*.

Love,

Lily   *Shelly* + Gil

Tad Poll   Minnie O.   Paddy

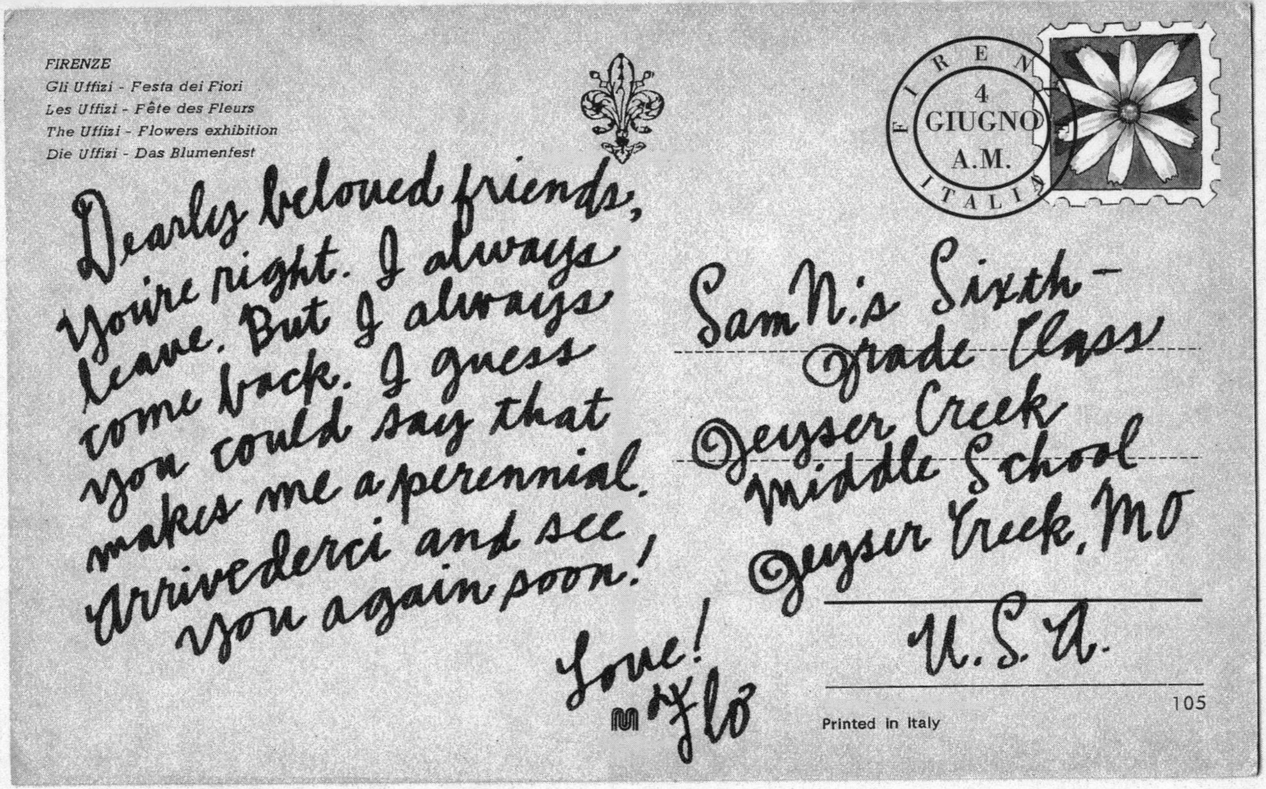
FIRENZE
Gli Uffizi - Festa dei Fiori
Les Uffizi - Fête des Fleurs
The Uffizi - Flowers exhibition
Die Uffizi - Das Blumenfest

FIRENZE
4
GIUGNO
A.M.
ITALIA

Dearly beloved friends,
You're right. I always
leave. But I always
come back. I guess
you could say that
makes me a perennial.
Arrivederci and see
you again soon!

Love!
Flo

Sam N.'s Sixth-
grade Class
Geyser Creek
Middle School
Geyser Creek, MO
U.S.A.

105

Printed in Italy

June 5

Florence Waters
My Treerific Friend
c/o Flowing Waters Fountains, Etc.
Florence, Italy

Dear Florence,

It was so fun to see you in Florence! Thanks for showing us around the most beautiful city in Italy.

I'm even more grateful to you for helping me save the trees here in Geyser Creek, especially the giant weeping willow. I know some people thought I was weird to care so much about that old tree. Then I returned from our trip and finished reading the minutes from the Maids of May meetings.

Florence, you're not going to believe what I discovered. I'll let you read the news for yourself. It's the very last entry in the Maids of May album. It was written 12 years ago. I know because ... that's how old I am.

　　　Minnie O.

MINUTES FROM THE MEETING OF THE MAIDS OF MAY

One member attended the May meeting, which did not begin with the customary composition or recitation of new verses to our pledge. I was simply too overwhelmed by events of late. I'll attach the newspaper article to explain.

THE DRY CREEK GAZ *12 YEARS AGO*

Thursday, April 29

nts

Car Accident Claims the Lives of Young Couple; Baby Survives

A tragic car accident last night claimed the lives of Olivia and Pierce Immon, both 24 years old and married just one year ago.

The accident occurred on westbound Creek Street when the couple lost control of their car. The vehicle reportedly rolled twice before colliding head-on into the weeping willow tree behind the middle school.

The couple's one-week-old daughter, Wilhomena, survived the crash. Witnesses said the baby was thrown from the vehicle into the boughs of the giant willow tree, which cradled the infant until emergency crews arrived on the scene. Doctors said the baby appeared frightened but unharmed.

The baby's mother, Olivia Immon, was the only child of Willow and Glen Forest, who passed away earlier this year. Olivia was the granddaughter of Wilhomena and Will U. Merrame, also deceased.

Olivia's husband, Pierce Immon, was also an only child. He was predeceased by his parents.

A native of Beijing, China, Pierce met Olivia at the University of Missouri, where he won dozens of awards for his poetry. Friends said he had been working on a collection of nature poems, which were also lost in the crash.

Olivia was an accomplished landscape architect. Like her parents and grandparents, she held her wedding under the weeping willow tree on the grounds of the middle school, where the bride, known to classmates as O., played as a child and celebrated her fifth birthday.

The couple's surviving baby will be cared for by Sandy Beech, who was Olivia's best friend dating back to their days at the University of Missouri, where the young women founded a chapter of the Maids of May.

Beech, now in her final year of medical school, not only served as maid of honor in Olivia's wedding, she also assisted in the delivery of her best friend's baby last week.

The late Olivia Immon named her daughter Wilhomena, after her grandmother Furr.

"Olivia planned to call her Minnie," said Beech. "But the baby looks so much like a miniature version of Olivia, I think I'll call her Minnie O."

Beech will begin adoption procedures immediately.

This concludes the business of the Maids of May.

Respectfully submitted,

Sandy Beech

Sandy Beech

Italian Branch Office
Florence, Italy

June 7

Minnie O.
12 Dogwood Trail
Geyser Creek, Missouri

Dear Minnie O.,

That tree saved your life! No wonder you were so
determined to save it. Your roots are there.

Just think: Your mother was a landscape architect.
That's why you have such respect for nature. And now
we know where your gift for writing comes from—your
father. Of course, your gift for saving lives comes from
your doctor mom. Think how proud all three would
be to call you their daughter!

Minnie O., you should be so proud of yourself for the
way you saved the trees. And this is only one of many
legacies you'll leave in your lifetime.

I wonder if *you* should write the minutes for the most
recent meeting of the Maids of May.

XO Florence

MINUTES FROM THE MEETING OF THE MAIDS OF MAY

For the first time in 12 years, the Maids of May held a meeting under the giant weeping willow tree at the prescribed time of 12:01 a.m. on May 1.

Actually, we met a few hours earlier because we had to decorate for the wedding. That's when Goldie told us the whole story about how she and Mr. N. had fallen in love, and how they (and not Florence and Wally) were getting married.

Many of the Maids of May were quite relieved by this news. The idea of Florence marrying Wally seemed, well, *freaky* to some of us. But when Florence arrived, she said that opposites often attract, and that Wally will make someone a wonderful husband someday—but she isn't that someone. Not today, anyway.

Well, everyone (except us!) was surprised at the ceremony when Mr. N. and Goldie exchanged vows instead of Florence and Wally. But even Florence was surprised when Chef Angelo asked Angel to marry him.

Speaking of surprised, maybe I should write about how Florence planted a giant hall tree inside our school, but why bother? Ask anybody who lives in Geyser Creek—or within 100 miles of here—and they'll tell you all about it. This will definitely go down in history as the best May Day ever!

I hope the founders of this esteemed society wouldn't mind that we included boys in our May Day celebration, as well as women who have married and divorced, and . . . well, just about anybody who wanted to join. At first I felt funny about changing the membership rules so drastically. But then I thought that times change, just like the seasons—and if anyone would understand that, the Maids of May would.

After we got back from our trip to Florence, Italy, I finished reading the minutes from the Maids of May meetings. That's when I discovered my real roots.

When I found out how my parents were killed in a car accident when I was just a week old, I told my mom I knew. She said she'd wanted to tell me herself for years but couldn't. Imagine: I lost my mother, but my mom lost her best friend. Mom said she and Olivia were more like sisters than friends.

It's still hard for Mom to talk about the accident without crying. Thinking about it sometimes makes me cry—not because I feel sad but because I feel loved.

Anyway, I decided to draw my family tree after all. And I trimmed it, too. But I didn't use a chainsaw! Instead, I trimmed my tree with all the people in my life who are like sisters and brothers and mothers and fathers and aunts and uncles to me.

Hey! Maybe that's why they're called family trees—because we can trim them any way we like.

Well, that's all I can think of to say. Wait. Maybe I'll write some final verses for the Maids Pledge.

> I am a Maid of May—
> At least I am today.
> Maybe someday I'll marry,
> But if I don't, that'll be a-okay.

> Like the Maids before me,
> I promise to root for trees.
> Because they remind me of my ancestry—
> And how we all try to leave a legacy.

Respectfully submitted,

Minnie O.

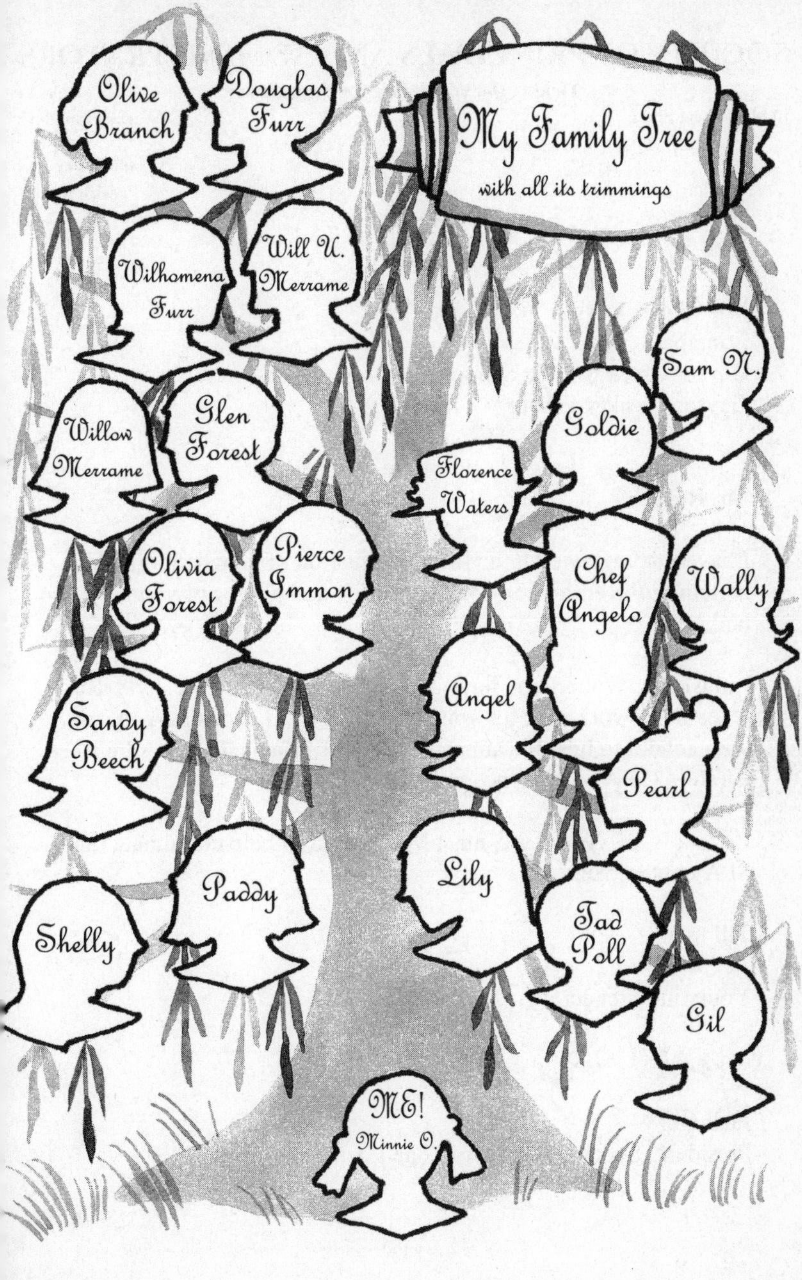
My Family Tree
with all its trimmings
Olive Branch
Douglas Furr
Wilhomena Furr
Will U. Merrame
Sam N.
Goldie
Willow Merrame
Glen Forest
Florence Waters
Olivia Forest
Pierce Immon
Chef Angelo
Wally
Angel
Sandy Beech
Pearl
Lily
Paddy
Shelly
Tad Poll
Gil
ME!
Minnie O.

SOCIETY OF PRINCIPALS AND ADMINISTRATORS

Making the World Safe for Bureaucracy

10 Maple Leaf Plaza

Washington, D.C.

Jack Oozy
President

June 7

Mr. Walter Russ
Principal
Geyser Creek Middle School
Geyser Creek, Missouri

Mr. Russ,

I have just reviewed Leif Blite's evaluation of your school,
including the entire correspondence file and photos of your new
hall tree.

I must say, Walter, you have an unusual administrative style. But
it seems to work well for you. That's why I'm choosing you and
your school to host the annual Society of Principals and Administrators (SPA) conference in August.

I strongly suggest you contact Ms. Waters to help coordinate the
SPA conference.

Till then,

Yours in bureaucracy,

Jack Oozy

Jack Oozy
President, Society of Principals and Administrators

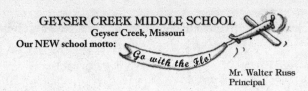

June 9

Ms. Florence Waters
President
Flowing Waters Fountains, Etc.
Watertown, California

Dear Ms. Waters,

Believe it or not, I passed my evaluation by the Society of Principals and Administrators (SPA). Needless to say, much of the credit goes to you.

I'm afraid to report that we have a new request. Is there any chance you might be available to help organize the first-ever SPA conference in Geyser Creek? Please advise.

Thank you for the hall tree. I'm really growing to like it. Though without a roof over my head, I worry a bit about winter.

Sincerely,

Walter

Walter Russ

P.S. In the confusion of May Day, I neglected to give you an "unwedding" present. Please know that this morning I planted a yew tree in your honor just outside my office window.

P.P.S. I must admit I really do love yew.

The Original Florence Court Yew

The Original Florence Court Yew
Florence Court, County Fermanagh

Cuttings from this single yew in Ireland are responsible for the millions of Irish yew in the world today. As such, the original Florence Court Yew is said to be the mother of all Irish yew.

FERMANAGH
12 JUNE A.M.
IRELAND

IRELAND

Wally,
A SRB conference? I'll bet this'll be fun. Oh right, this research is new and much a Weir and behind much a Meir far behind. Oh over there. I'll see you soon. Thanks again Wally.

Wally Knox
Princing Pal
Geyser Creek
Middle School
Geyser Creek,
Mont
U.S.A.

CLASSROOM ACTIVITIES FOR REGARDING THE TREES

LANGUAGE

- The Italian lessons throughout this book get longer and more complicated. As a class, try saying some of the phrases. If there are foreign-language speakers in your class, have them teach some of the same basic words and phrases in another language. Are any of the words similar to English words in the way they are spelled or the way they sound?

- Minnie O.'s slogan, "Ax not! It's what you can do for your country . . .'" (p. 60) is a parody of a passage from President John F. Kennedy's inauguration speech. Locate an audio version of this speech for your class and play it aloud, or provide a transcript. How are Minnie O.'s words different from President Kennedy's? Is the meaning the same?

- Homonyms are used frequently in this book and others in the series. For example, the word *graft* is used in this book (pp. 19, 68–70), but it is not used the same way each time. Have each student keep a list of homonyms and note how the usage of each varies as they read. Encourage the students to use context clues to determine which definition of the word is appropriate for each situation in the story.

SOCIAL STUDIES

- Assign each student the task of mapping and illustrating his or her family tree, or the family tree of friends, as Minnie O. does (pp. 140–41).

- The Geyser Creek sixth graders learn that the flowering dogwood is the state tree of Missouri (p. 22). Every state has a designated tree, flower, bird, and other highlighted plants, animals, and natural resources. As a class, conduct research to identify your home state's official tree, flower, bird, or other specified symbols. Discuss why these symbols were chosen to represent your state.

SCIENCE

- As a class, explore the school grounds. Observe the trees and plants growing around the school. Make a map of the grounds and mark each tree's location. Collect a leaf from each tree to use to identify the tree when you return to the classroom. Make sure to note which tree each leaf came from so the tree can be labeled on the map.

- As a class, choose one tree on the school grounds to observe for a season. During that season, write down in a class science log all changes the tree undergoes, such as leaf color, bird or insect activity, limb loss, and seasonal changes.

Find a free teacher's guide for all of the books in the series online at **www.HarcourtBooks.com/Guides.**

Author **Kate Klise** (left) and illustrator **M. Sarah Klise** are sisters and collaborators. Together they have created many TREEmendous books for young readers, including four other books in the Regarding the . . . series, *Letters from Camp, Trial by Journal,* and the picture books *Shall I Knit You a Hat?: A Christmas Yarn, Why Do You Cry?,* and *Imagine Harry.* While working on this book, Kate planted three redbuds, two dogwoods, and one weeping willow tree in her little valley near Norwood, Missouri. Sarah, meanwhile, prudently pruned the lemon tree that grows behind her house in Berkeley, California.

To learn more about the Klise sisters, visit their website at **www.kateandsarahklise.com.**

Research Your Family Tree

What are your roots? Research your family tree and find out.

① Start by writing <u>Your Name</u> at the bottom of the tree.

② If you have <u>Brothers</u> and <u>Sisters</u>, add their names.

③ Put your <u>Parents</u> above your siblings.

④ Don't forget your <u>Aunts</u> and <u>Uncles</u>.

⑤ Grandparents are next.

⑥ Aren't <u>Great-Grandparents</u> great? Add 'em now.

Interview older relatives. Ask them to share funny family stories.